POLLUTO.

Polluto is published four times a year by Dog Horn Publishing. Visit polluto.com or doghorn.com to subscribe or for submission details.

T0316008

Editor-in-Chief: Adam Lowe
Acquisitions Editor: Victoria Hooper
Creative Director: Michael Dark
Artist-in-Residence: Dave Migman

CULTure supplement available online as free download or in print for a small fee.

Dog Horn Publishing
6 Athlone Terrace
Armley
Leeds
LS12 1UA
United Kingdom

A copyright record for this title exists with Nielsen BookData/Bowker and the British Library.

If you enjoyed this title, please share it with your friends.

POLLUTO.

EDITOR'S LETTER

Well, here it is . . . Issue 5. A little late, but here, goddamnit! We've also tweaked the formula a little. For instance, you'll notice this issue is much heftier than any of the preceding issues. Also, you'll notice there's no artwork inside. This is us playing with the formula a bit, and shouldn't worry you too much. The artwork will instead be available in our online *CULTure* supplement, which can be printed off and kept or purchased direct from our site at cost price. Subscribers will get the *CULTure* supplement for free, which is an added incentive to subscribe.

CONTENTS

Millions Must Die	Dave Migman	p.3
Porcelain and Chrome	J. Michael Shell	p.5
The Spectacle	Kristina Marie Darling	p.9
Treason Is	Forrest Aguirre	p.11
A Steampunk Orange	Deb Hoag	p.15
What Women Want	Philippa Bower	p.20
Exchange	Helena Thompson	p.23
Sheep Shagging	Dave Migman	p.27
Pink	Miles Klee	p.29
Nine Days:		
The Stone Boy's Lament	Kurt Kirchmeier	p.48
Mud Wrestling		
in a Distant Land	Marshall Payne	p.52
Life's Necessities	Deborah Walker	p.55
Leviathan's Teeth	Kelly Barnhill	p.64
In the Dutiful Republic	Terence Kuch	p.78
Home is Where		
the Heart Is	Mark Howard Jones	p.80
Anarchy in the UK	Micci Oaten	p.95
Clowning Around	Jon Peck	p.99
Clash of Cultures	Steve Redwood	p.109

POLLUTO.

Free Choice	Dave Migman	p.120
It's Fear	Dave Migman	p.121
Magnet Dragged It	Dave Migman	p.123
Circle and Djinn	Robert Lamb	p.124
Silent Treatment	Erik Williams	p.137
Sandy Stravinsky's Best Date Ever	William Peacock	p.149
Future Shock	Tom Sanchez Prunier	p.156
The Copper Heart	Drew Rhys White	p.159
Vasty Deep	Ren Holton	p.175
Cancer	Fred Venturini	p.201

MILLIONS MUST DIE

DAVE MIGMAN

there are 2 paths the species can take. the 1st is the oldest. already ingrained into the circuitry like dirt in the whorls of your fingers.

the first then is the Imminent Path Into Extinction.

but let's go back in time and introduce Nohj. Nohj says "I believe we are all one, one unit, many diffrent colours and flavours but we're essentially all one." pulls on his spliff "And we need to realise that and stop the fighting and fooling about and realise our potentiality."

"But we're not 'all at one'. we're dissolute, always at each others throats, in the past My tribe fought Your tribe because Your tribal diety's face looked diffrent. The conflicts only escalate as populations increase. The more horrific they become as technology 'progresses'. But it's hardwired in. It is in our souls, our chemical biological make-up. to attack, to hate—violence! to say that we're all one . . . well that's pretty damned naive."

he looks across at me. tired of talking now. but you get my point. the path has been long set since the first cave man pushed a splintered bone through another caveman's chest

the second path is Nohj's naive path: Complete Species Enlightenment—to attain the universal harmony of spirit, an awakening of human conciousness to educate and work on what matters, what creates war, the 'bloodflow lust'. to attain such a stance 'millions would have to die' the world would be a charnel house of those that wouldn't put down their guns and swords, the earth would be soggy with the entrails at our feet. how could we live or 'enhance' ourselves with such a conscience weighing us?

there is a third factor here. not a path . . . not as such. It is a predetermined route, that as subjects of nature we submit to Her whim and are incapable of controlling such fiery or so--called negative emotions. That Nature itself evokes the warlike node inside us as a way of controlling numbers. This path is the Route from Her Womb and the fruit it shall bloom long after we are gone.

THE END

PORCELAIN AND CHROME

J. MICHAEL SHELL

He wore a chrome flash-drive hung about his neck on a fine silver chain. At night, he took it off and laid it into the outreaching arms of a porcelain angel perched atop a small, cedar chest-of-drawers. The angel was beautiful—all white with gilt highlights and mother-of-pearl wings. Though he appreciated her beauty, he was not fond of her. At night, she protected his only treasure in accordance with their unspoken understanding that he would smash her to shards if she didn't. Other than that protection, he had no use for her kind. The beauty of angels, he knew, was subject to declination when they fell (unless, of course, you fall with them—then beauty is truly in the eye of the beholder).

When it was hung upon his breast, that small, rectangular piece of memory was more a true cross than any such icon ever worn by priest or bishop or pope. He could feel its weight bending him like Christ's own tree. On warm days it stuck to his sternum and threatened to melt through into his chest. At times, the burden of it was so great that he imagined raising a hammer to smash it. But in those fantasies, he *could not* bring that hammer down. Even imagining such a thing would have broken the cold chrome his heart had become. At night, he laid that representation of his heart onto the angel's arms and wound its chain twice around her wrists.

◊

Thirty years ago there were no such devices, but still he'd been shackled to what it now carried. In cardboard boxes filled with the smell of ink and carbon, he stored the very same memories—memories of places and things and people and events that had and hadn't been. Memories of personalities and psyches and egos. Memories of erotic diversions and infantile omniscience.

Back then, these memories occasionally became lost. Paper was a poor and fragile medium. Mechanical manuscripts were hard to produce and correct and copy. But, to him, they'd been much more real—produced entirely by the exertions of sinew. Electricity, back then, only aided creation within one's brain.

◊

Eventually, those paper chains fell onto discs housed in thin plastic squares. Electricity had been set loose, and was lighting up monitors, processing words. Processing. But when he'd finally processed all his old ink-pounded paper into boxes full of these discs, and put every new memory and thought and creation in there with the old, electricity evolved once again. Into the chrome flash-drive all that weight fell, like angels diving off heads of pins—like light spiraling into singular darkness. Like a universe condensing. He wore it around his neck by day, and bound the angel with it at night.

◊

Winter, it seemed, was the hardest season. In winter, the chrome felt icy on his chest. He wished he could wear it outside his shirt, but knew that would be tantamount to sacrilege. True penance needs the involvement of flesh, as do retribution and tribulation. The precious chill of those shell-cased memories reminded him that he loved them too much, called them up too frequently. Then, one night, that frost seeped into him so deeply that anger formed on his brow like a glacier. As he took off his amulet, he looked down at the angel with her outreaching arms and for the first time noticed that her barely smiling lips were red. No other color, save the gold leaf lit highlights and the mother-of-pearl glazing, adorned her. How could he never have noticed this before? "Where did you get those lips?" he said aloud, and he could have sworn her Mona Lisa smile widened just a breath. "You bitch," he told her, that cold anger congealing on him.

Squinting his eyes, he bent closer to her tiny face. She was immensely beautiful—glamorous in the true sense of the word, especially with that blood-red rouge accenting her lips. "When you fall, you'll grow fangs," he told her as he laid the cold chrome onto her arms. Then he wound the chain around her wrists, not twice as had become his custom, but again and again, until she was bound tight with the full length of that silver cord. A strange excitement swelled in him as he looked at her tied like that. A smile, induced by some erotic spark of electricity in his brain, captured his lips and held them. Even as he fell into bed and turned out the light, that smile would not release him.

◊

Whether it was before or after he'd fallen asleep is, perhaps, a matter of genre. Either way, the occasion of her standing full grown and fleshly at the foot of his bed was as real to him as any dream is to its dreamer. With her arms outstretched toward him, her face fell into sadness and pleading. Even without speaking, her plea was obvious, as the chain about her wrists dripped blood from where it cut her. Cupped into her delicate hands, she held his chrome clad memory. "You want me to release you," he told her, sitting up in his bed.

"*Release,*" she said, though it sounded like an echo.

"What will you give me?" he asked, that smile once again creeping down from his brain.

"Give *me,*" she echoed, and a hint of smile on her *own* face bared a brilliant tooth.

◊

Slowly he unwound the chain that bound those pale, alabaster hands. When it was done, he saw the deep purple bruises gilt with blood from where the chain had cut her. This sight affected him strangely as well, and he felt more sparks arousing him.

Taking her by those abused wrists, he pulled her into his bed and on top of him. Her angel body was hot and molten soft. Looking down at him, she smiled fully—revealing her porcelain teeth. As she smiled, he slid a finger onto her tongue, which was red as her lips. When she closed her mouth and wrapped her tongue around his finger, he pushed it in till it reached the back of her throat.

As he did this, he thought she was echoing his gesture with her own finger, and he took it deep into his mouth. But just as he began to swallow, he realized what she had done. Too late to stop it, he pushed her away as the chrome flash-drive slid down his throat, followed by its chain.

As the last inch of chain was passing over his lips, the angel snatched it between her pretty fingers. A tremendous smile, more like a silent roar, revealed how sharp her teeth really were. With her own mouth, she motioned for him to open his wide. When he did, she pulled on the chain—delicately choking him as she once again smiled hugely. Even in his tormented state, he noticed how terribly beautiful she became as she tugged on his burden again and again, then watched him swallow it back down.

THE END

THE SPECTACLE

KRISTINA MARIE DARLING

THE SPECTACLE

It was the night of his first performance and the audience had arrived. Each of the gentlemen,

magnificent in pinstripes and a red silk tie, seemed ready to bare his teeth. And while the men

tapped their feet, waiting for a grandiloquent concerto to begin, even the arched brows of the

women seemed to threaten. *Yet there is something inherently carnivorous about an audience,* the

musician thought as the lights dimmed. He struck the first chord. The ladies, gathering their long

blue skirts, were the first to rise.

THE TENOR

It's evenings like these I think he's singing again, all diaphragm and gusto, his arms outstretched with the dark blue notes of *La Bohème*. Even the crystal begins to hum. Yet when the chorus

starts up, crooning languidly into the greenish night, a colorless moon hangs speechless in every

window. The only sound—a beveled mirror shuddering in its frame. Then the room grows still

like a little bell chiming on the hour.

HÔTEL DIEU

When the dark green eaves of the opera house loomed above her, the old woman was right to be

afraid. Because she had never noticed the hurricane lamps in the windows before, or the way

they smoldered in the fog. *And tonight,* she thought, *my heart will empty out like a bottle of milk*

and drift away . . . An usher waited near the door, grinning in his red velvet suit. The halls behind

him were dim and twisted like the neck of a harp.

TREASON IS

FORREST AGUIRRE

The man in the iron dunce cap sat hunched in his chair, chest and chin flat to the wooden desk, unable to lift his loden head. His hand, a sentient being, connected to his body, it seemed, only through the following movement of his eyes, scrawled furiously, charcoal scratches materializing on the papyrus beneath his etiolated digits:

Word, as the proto-object, the ur-core, creates meaning. There is no meaning without Word. Self-conscious-ness is subservient to Word, as Word is necessary to describe "self-conscious". Word is essence. The meaning of essence comes from Word.

A guard entered daily, the hollow clank of key on lock a signal that the man with the iron dunce cap must lift his hand for a new sheaf of paper. He was fed through a needle in his neck. Day in, day out, the nutrient soup drip-dripped into his anemic bloodstream, his face devoid of emotion, his body slack, only the eyes and hand moving, writing, creating meaning, the Word.

At night he thought. He remembered. He thought he remembered the night when he was brought to this place. A word, "treason," blazed in his thoughts when he thought of *before* this place. Sometimes, if the moonbeams shone at just the right angle and reflected from his burdensome cap, he would write at night:

> Treason, as the proto-action, the ur-verb, creates meaning. There is no meaning without treason. Self-conscious-ness is subservient to treason, as treason is necessary to describe "self-conscious".
> Treason is essence. The meaning of essence comes from treason.

It was on those glowing nights, when his head cast a conical shadow on the granite prison wall behind him, that hope welled up in his sunken chest.

Hope, with thoughts of treason, all intertwined into a shimmering utopian vision of the future, the details blurred, like a view of the full moon from under water, the drowning man desperate to surface for air.

◊

The narrow cobble streets of the shingle-roofed city erupted in violence. "The King-men must die!" the crowds chanted. Nobles sans noblesse slinked shirtless through back alleys, hid in treasure chests, even cast themselves from palatial windows, self-defenestrating to avoid the humiliation of public beheading. Royal privilege allowed them to take their lives by suicide before the common rabble apprehended them—decorum demanded it. This robbed the mob of its satisfaction: Long die the king!

◊

No one came in to remove the sheafs from under the man in the dunce cap. He remained forgotten for days. He might have died save for the dripping vein-fed fluid entering his neck. When the moonlight shined through to his cell —in reality it was sunlight filtered through the smoke of burning castles and corpses. But the man had no sense of time in his cell—when a ghostly shimmer *which happened to be* moonlight to his weary eyes suffused his prison crown—he was compelled to write; words superimposed over one another in a melange:

> Word, as the proto-meaning, the ur-con-sciousness, creates trea-son. There is no treason without meaning. Self-treason is conscious to Word, as consciousness is necessary to describe "self-Word". Treason is conscious essence. The meaning of consciousness comes from treason. Smoke . . .

"Smoke" because it was at that moment that his olfactory sense became aware of a smell other than rust and mildew and rat fur.

He assayed to scribble more (preparing to write on his suspicions regarding the confluence of senses, the nerve batch where smoke-smell and charcoal-feel meet) but was interrupted by the clanking of a key inside his cell-door's lock. Many voices followed the creaky door, flooding the room with the scent of ashes on clothing. None of the voices were that of the guard.

◊

The crowd hoisted him up on their shoulders, careful to brace the break-neck cap, and carried him through the streets. The strain on his neck from years of wearing his burden had set his jaw locked and bearded chin splintered—when they asked for a speech he merely smiled and waved. It was enough. Cheers erupted at his lolling nod, subsided at his lifted hand.

He was brought into the old throne room—charred and plundered, save for the jewel-encrusted seat on which they set him. His head lolled back, the iron cap settling into the soft gold, bending it until crumpled resistance held it aloft at an odd angle, craning his neck in a resting pose where he might look over the throne room at his subjects.

His last sheaf of writings was framed in exotic woods by his followers (he still could not remember *why* they followed him, but felt it had something to do with his clouded utopian visions), then nailed above and behind his throne. But because of the iron dunce cap (which, he learned by feel, was embossed with a large "T") he was unable to turn and see the holy artifact. He had difficulty remembering the words on the wall.

◊

One day (or night? There were no windows in the throne room.) a large man, half again the new ruler's stature and several times his weight, entered the throne room. He was not a happy man. "I was the dead king's bodyguard" he declared as he swung back an immense bloodied maul (evidence for why the guards were not responding). The instrument came full-force across the dunce's cap, separating it from the new ruler's head.

◊

After the assassination, experts came to interpret the new red writing on the manifesto above the erstwhile ruler's corpse. Philosophical debate spawned disagreements and arguments, blossom- ing, once again, into riot on the city's narrow streets. The corpse sat smiling, his head trickling words down the velvet throne and on to the floor. Treason, once again, had meaning.

THE END

A STEAMPUNK

ORANGE

DEB HOAG

Fookin' rozzer," I said, me Lexie, and I scanned him as he jacked concrete down the sidewalk in his oversize metal kickers. I was sittin' in myshop, minding my own, a little of the old in-and-out doing with my sticker and inks.

"Coming here?" asked the icy little bird who had put herself under my wing, spread her skin, her palette wide in front of my stinging brushes.

I pushed harder with the sticker and watched the blood bead up. "We'll find out soon enough, if the Great Angel makes his way in here, won't we?" She flittered the glassies at me and wrigged around so I got a better view of her groodies, but it was the bright beading blood that I watched.

Then the door opened and the rozzer swaggered in, and the icy bird tired to fold her wings, but I put up a knee so she stayed spread, thinkin that if I had to carf with the rozzer, at least I was on my feet and not bleedin'. They can smell the bright scarlet bead like a mingin' nonce can smell a sixpence twat.

He scannered me shop like I'd numpty that he was looking for inkers for that broad rozzer skin, all fat and delirious on the red-meat in steroid sauce they feed 'em. His scanners lit on me visage real casual-like, as if he were just skimpering down the street with no purpose ahead whatsoever.

"'Allo, there," he said, all beneficent like. "Mebe you can give me some aid, here."

"Done give at the scarlet bank," I said, which caused the bird to giggle and earned her a scan that singed her feathers quick.

"Ye don't know what I'm in aid of yet, unless you're a friggin' jidder, now, do ye?" He circled me shop with his glassies, then rounded back to run them over me like the old oozy me mother used creech about.

"You may be a Great Angel to the kinglies up top, but there ain't much any rozzer'd dance here for except pinning some gormless spaz to the brick. I ain't got no call to be pinned. Is it he bird?" I gave her a surprised scanner, then back to the rozzer, who was squaring up his tucker fiercely. "Is it that she's a skinner then? A buller? Will you take her in chains out my plain little door?"

The bird chirped and I twisted the sticker, just to shut her tucker.

"Somebody got skinnered, all right, but it weren't no downside skozzer."

"Well, then, who was it, Oh my brother? I don't know nothing about any skinner, skozzer or not."

I scanned his face as I was speakin' and saw his scanners pinch and his puddin' go white when I called him brother. I could hear a little bell, tink, tank clinkering in me head, a warning song that rang from hear to hear. Did he grok, then who my donor was? Bio dad, where art thou, was that the question the rozzers were scraping for the answer to?

17

"Time then, your little bird flew home, I'm thinkin'," he poked, and I pulled the sticker and jerked her out. She was creechin' about her art, and after all, she took a slap to the puddin' to get her out the door.

I locked the door and turned to give him the cold scanner. He scanned back, then twisted his tucker into shark-smile. "It were me old droog, name o' Dim. A week ago it was a soddin' judy head nozzer what used to work in the state hotel, it were. A handful before that, someone tried to tanker down me other droog, Pete. Now, what do you t grok that me and me old mates had in common with a kinglie like the doctor? Onliest one thing that comes to mind, and I hear you're the livin' prrof he ever existed."

I shrugged, and kept my scanners tight. "I heard that tinkling, too," I said. "But I count where the polly flows from, Great Angel, and ain't none flowed from that river, no more than black and suds flows from me mother's groodies."

"She's gormless. I went there first. Don't as know her fanny from her nozzer, that much I scannered before I was all the way in the door."

Shrug-speak again. Did he want me to answer, he should query the interrogatory plain.

"The donor's been dead for two decs," I said, making to put the bird's polly in the lock box.

Big meat-rooker slamming on the counter, scary-sort, but I didn't even bother to scanner. Yawned me tucker wide, like I was ready to nod, his tinkle was so flat.

"We dug 'em up."

Now I was jumpin' and working to keep me visage iced. "You dug up the old worm food? Wot fookin' for? Ta ask him who done it? Tip for the rozzers: I don't think he knows."

The Great Angel, who I knew now must be General Georgie, scannered around the shop for a minute, decidin' what tale to whisper in me hear. Finally, he scannered back on me. "DNA. Didn't have it when he tried to fly off the building.

18

Landed right on his tucker and kissed it good. Right hair, right window, right pan-handle in his trou. Fookin' him, I woulda sworn it. DNA says no. Fancy that. Two decs and people start dyin. Figure him or you, you bein' the only spot 'o juice we know of that stook to the wall."

I crinkled my scanners at him. "Me? I'm a lolly bird, ye nit. Half a scratch above a slag, when I need the polly to keep the stick-shop open."

The meat-rook landed on me groodie, and I got the shark-smile glimmed back. "And how much polly der it take then, little slag? I got a hankerin' to frig me old droog's chicka. Maybe nothing for your old uncle Georgie, eh, darlin'? Just to keep it all in the fam, so to speak."

I was nearly gaggin' at the fry oilin' whif of him, and reachin for the big sticker I kept under the counter. But then dear ole dad came swingin' up behind, and swang like he was still in the horrowshow, and I clapped me rookers when the rozzer fell.

When the rozzer came to, he was strapped to the sticker seat, and I had the long stickin' bit to put the ink all over him. He sputtered awake all indig like, as if I gave a fookin' pence what his patter was while I was stripping skin and pushin' ink. Me old dad sat on a perch right near, watching as I pushed "Traitor Shite" across his chest. And viz. Fat meat poles ran with blood and ink.

While I worked, dad gave him the enlightenment about the gormer that really tried to fly out the window, and me old da's search for restoration from the state friggin his nozzer. "Took me nearly two decs to find someone as could put me nozzer back the way it was," he tinked, catchin' up on the ole, as it were. "Now here I am, playin' with me old droogies, like time never was, Georgie. Scarpin' fun enough to dance to, ain't it?"

Dad made his point by snuffin' it out his stick in the bright rushing blood. Rushin' up to greet me like an old droog. When he stopped screamin' at the snuffwork, I 'd know he was termed.

Dad scannered while I stuck—good crit, him. He hit the player and we listened to the glorious rising spark of Ludvig, who vizzed the heavens and caught them in crystal. It took some power volly to drown the creeching, and the glass was shaking to the bass. We pulled more of the rozzer's cancers while I pushed inn the grace notes, then rose together as he lay bubbling and leavin' bead by bead, bound to the stickin' chair.

Dad put his rooker around me shoulders as we locked tight and left. "Shame to lose the sticker shop," I said.

"One more old droog to gift, then done and skatin' off, we'll be. Sing a merry tune, then, will ya, Lexie, darling?" Dad said.

I gave him a viz full of familial love.

"I grok that I'm behind the times, luv," Dad said thoughtfully. "I been hearing the tinkle. When we scatter, you can catch me up and teach me all about the steampunk and the new terror polly, eh? What a pair we'd make, draggin' shooters and nippin' the grand republicrat."

"Too fookin' cold here, anyhow." I looked back at General George, appreciatin' him much better doornailed as creeching. "He was my best piece."

Dad's hand slipped down and squeezed me arse with heartstrings tinkling loud enough to ring my hears. General Georgie was right. Keep it in the fam, luv.

WHAT WOMEN WANT

PHILIPPA BOWER

Betsie Brown hummed happily while she dusted the photo frames on her mantelpiece. Fifteen lovely grand-children and another on the way—she would soon be running out of space for all the pictures. She looked around her neat little living room. Tomorrow she would beeswax the furniture and polish the wood into a deep gleam, but today she didn't have time—she had to go and see the doctor. Betsie took off her apron, checked her tightly-curled grey hair in the mirror, put on her coat and set off for the clinic.

As she walked down the road she noted with approval the houses where the nets were white and the windows shone. Judging others against her own high standards was a habitual pleasure. Knockers polished, doorsteps scrubbed, gardens weeded—there was nothing like good housekeeping to make a nice neighbourhood. Sometimes, like a bad tooth in a smiling mouth, there was an uncared-for house belonging to a Working Woman. Betsie regarded Working Women with a contempt that was tinged with envy that they should care so little for appearances.

A young woman drove past in a silver sports car, her loose blonde hair blowing in the wind. For a moment Betsie wondered what it would be like to experience such freedom—to be able to drive a car, to have one's own money, to come and go at will and not be reliant on her husband for everything. What was she thinking? She was shocked by her disloyalty. Frank and the children—and now the grandchildren, were everything to her. Why should she want freedom? She was worried by the strange thoughts she had been having lately, that, and the sharp pain at the top of her nose.

Betsie sat in the doctor's surgery. Her bright gaze surveyed the doctor—a Working Woman. The doctor's bloused was creased, her collar un-starched, her shoes had not been polished for a while. She looked up from her notes and her eyes were tired.

"What can I do for you Mrs Brown?"

"I have a pain in my nose."

"Tilt your head back please, let's have a look." The doctor picked up a penlight torch and shone it up Betsie's nostril. "Ah yes, there seems to be something blocking your nasal passage. Have you been poking things up your nose Mrs Brown?"

"No I have not." Betsie was affronted. The doctor rummaged in a drawer and brought out a pair of long, slender tweezers.

"It should be easy enough to remove," she said, and gently slid the tweezers up Betsie's nose. "Ah, got it," She gave a tug. "It seems to be attached."

"Ouch," said Betsie. The obstruction came away. The doctor pulled it out and held it up triumphantly—it looked like a small, square cornflake.

"What is it?" asked Betsie, dabbing with a clean, white handkerchief at the blood and mucous dripping out of her nose.

"It's a Stepford chip," the doctor stared at it in fascination. "It must have been put into you about thirty years ago."

"Who would do such a thing?"

"The Government. They chipped a whole generation of women to make them stay at home."

"But why?"

"In those days the population was plummeting and children were running wild. Something drastic had to be done."

"Have you got a chip?" Betsie asked the doctor.

"Of course not," the doctor dismissed the thought impatiently and returned to her exposition. "The problem was solved, but by a gross violation of human rights. The Stepford project had to be hushed up." For a moment the doctor looked angry, and then she turned to Betsie with a bright smile. "But never mind Mrs Brown, your body has rejected the chip—you have the chance to fulfil your potential and live for yourself instead of living for others."

Her enthusiasm was contagious and Betsie realised that the pleasure she had taken in little acts of creativity had been misplaced. The cakes and jam and hand-knitted jerseys that had been so appreciated by family and friends could more easily have been bought. Instead of caring for her possessions she could have been replacing them—if only she had been a Working Woman. The doctor was about to throw the Stepford chip into the disposal bin, when Betsie had a thought and stopped her.

"What are you having for dinner tonight, doctor?" she asked. The doctor ran a distracted hand across her forehead to brush away an untidy strand of hair.

"I hadn't thought," she said. "I might buy a takeaway or take a pizza out of the freezer. Why?"

Betsie thought of the delicious, home-made steak-and-kidney pudding waiting in the oven at home; and Frank's pleasure when she presented him with his favourite meal on his return from work. She held her head high.

"Please doctor, I would like you to put the chip back in again."

THE END

EXCHANGE

HELENA THOMPSON

Talking to you **if whatever we say**
slow dawning babe every *word* you are my
my mothering seems to **should hacknify**
we'll laugh at horizon spanning *betray*
space above my eyes and limbs **the cliche**
which tickles our lips *what was that I missed?*
A stumbling my matter it *until kissed*
syllabol a *it sooths itself away...*
imagination **heart** might *needed no*
information moderate **to make you**
what she made you beat—*a beauty that grows*
accommodate **and what did Judas do?**
for so many *(now some and* **silver sleights;**
warm gesture without words) subdue you quite.

ILLUSION

HELENA THOMPSON

SEROTONIN HELD MY EYES AGAPE I
Here I lie CHEWED ON ROLLING WORDS recall

those *MADE A PRODUCT NOW in a half lie*
WHAT CAN'T I *empty whole against the wall.*
DO? LOVE ME YOU SAID AND HOW (PUPILS PILL
WOUNDED) I WISHED YOU HAD COMMANDED gentle
*OF WHAT YOU WERE (*IRISES CONGEALED STILL)
MY THOUGHT DEVICES CONVENIENT pencil
LIKE MY LIPS HAD *AS READY PREPARED MEALS*
(A DOUBLE NEGATIVE) NEVER *NO LESS*
UNSATISFYING YET MOVED strokes tracing
my form like fingers; in that (head racing
to heavy wait) suspended still (*YES YES*
I KNOW IT IS)IT WAS I was made real.

THE WEST IS DONE

DAVE MIGMAN

the
West dissolves into the promise
of its repose blood feud and orgies
a cross between convicts sucking out
juices feaces blood and semen
a new social contract soiled by
snuff terroist peadophiles under age
girls and boys sticking it to each other
the 'new teen sex addicts' fuck like
rabbits between doses of adverts 'how to

POLLUTO.

improve your sex appeal'—dress less
the elders're worthless media mogul conspirators
bear their allegience in their palms transfer
this logo to your flesh the brand be
good don't cross the line into radicalism
bearded anarchist madmen Bin Laden fascists
Islamic moneylender lefty commie ENEMY
always, indelible, a brand name—THEMselves
the empire of rats, the nation of pampered,
bored elite, cushion happy oh god
my hair disaster oh god bleach the
flesh white is still success ah
this fickle reflection, flicker morality
our lack of control in a society thus
controlled the veneer of the tome, saviours
politics and preachers back home to
abuse the system in the system above
the system above the law but lower
no!

snorting up primeland
the remainder for gravel pits now the farming's
done. A playground for the rich turfing
out the weeds and send them to the city
some inner hovel box on box with
a twenty year lifespan for this consummerist
wet dream.

fortress Britain overrun by

POLLUTO.

Blairite Thatcherite *pure bullshite*
hammerhead business expanding lust,
grow, prosper
out of control so it's crazy, feeding
the beast full of waste.

cities so fat on it they spew out
their entrails into the country. Each
one a virulant sore chewing on the
Goddess cunt sticking out more lights
to block out the moon's original
glow, more toxins to choke
more things to fill our bins more
more so we stand in lines glaring
at the checkout sow cursing queues
consumerism plastic bags
but we're all in it, fill them it's easier
that way, to fill the hate,
to keep away. Disengage. The Dream.

night now, quiet now, between them
humming computers, the breath of
transference

data spiders
stranded behind cupboards.

SHEEP SHAGGING

DAVE MIGMAN

She says "You don't believe in Heaven?"
voice rising, modulation like trumpets
cross section, like this is the middle
ages—like the sweat of visionaries,
poets, warriors; the blood that oozes
though the philosopher's stone the tears
that turned to diamonds before they
shattered on the floors of fractured ideas
amongst hordes *and still she clings to this!*
"No, think I'll go for passive
re-incarnation: I know I should advance
but there's something I should do here."
"You believe we come back? that's pure crazy!"
"You believe in angels!"
"That's different, the Bible's different, it's a book."
"Ever read it?"
"No, but, I was taught it."
"Ah, selective knowledge."
blinking.
I push in, to the hilt,
she gasps a little noonooo
which translates as yes please fuck me,
and we continue the dance. No words

POLLUTO.

this time, just the need to consume

each others lust and loneliness. This

little Christian clutching her wooden 'fix

like a child

a sugar mouse

PINK

MILES KLEE

W hen we were old enough, the pool started bleeding. Byron noticed, adrift in shade on my shark floater: an acorn hit him on the head and he'd opened his eyes to find it bobbing in the water, ribbons of red uncoiling beneath. Came and got me and I got mom and she got dad.

"It's not blood," mom said, squinting. "What is it."

"Not blood," dad agreed.

No swimming till our pool guy Darren gave the OK. Byron and Mackenzie fought on the rock waterfall while he worked, Kenz pulling up her bikini top every four seconds for tanline checks, Byron plugging the spout with his foot for fields of spray, gagging when he glimpsed the Runt's flatness. That + Darren's screaming equipment + Berkie pawing the door to go out were fucking up this annoying Mozart piece, and just as I banged the piano shut Kenzie materialized, dripping on hardwood. She did her who-wouldn't-love-this smile, ran a tongue over top teeth. The braces were finally gone, but not the nightmares: threaded metal tightening, the crank where gum and bone pulled apart.

"Can you beat Byron up?"

He almost won (we'll be the same size again soon, but he still looks like my botched clone), and I took the injury, a black eye even mom asked about. *Already said, Tinman whanged me with his axe in rehearsal.* Anyway, I pushed Byron into the water when he thought it was over.

"You're not supposed to!" Kenzie wailed. Byron heaved himself onto the deck, sputtering.

"I *know*," he went, and rubbed where I bit him.

Darren came out to collect his stuff and said your standard red algae, killable with chemicals. Daddo doesn't check the pH too often, does he, he laughed.

"Nah," said Byron, shivering in my towel, "but I give it a litmus test now and then."

◊

Neuter Your Pet Weekend at Barker Field: drop them with lab-coated people at the turnstiles, pick them up fixed after. We had put off doing Berkie long enough. Took baseball gloves and crammed into the backseat. Dad came out alone and started the car.

"Can I sit up front, then?" Kenz asked, but we were already moving.

"Factory was going crazy last night," Byron said.

"What factory."

"You don't hear? It goes whoooooofff. *krang*!" He shook his whole face; his cheeks swung where he'd lost the fat. Mackenzie squealed. I made my own noise. She reminded me I wasn't funny. I kept at it, and she sang Spice Girls to drown me out. By the time Berkie started howling, dad had to pull over.

The ballpark, by the way, had *only* neutering. Spay Day was a week before, and did we expect them to babysit our mutt for three hours? So we piled back in the car, came home and found mom in an Adirondack by the hot tub having a gin and tonic with Darren. They looked at us and down at the pool deck. At a soggy broken squirrel piled on a bed of pink splatter. Clods of dirty grass and a single acorn for garnish. It was dusk but the underwater lights were off.

"Algae strikes again," said Byron.

"Deep in the filter," Darren explained, "missed it at first."

"Where's your father?" asked mom. "Game over so soon?"

Kenzie cried because a cute thing died, then said she was PMSing and didn't want dinner.

"Nobody's making you," I said.

"And you don't have PMS," Byron added, scratching his balls.

Dad came out with a beer. Darren fiddled with his crappy State U visor, told him these accidents come with the territory: animals get disoriented, follow the lights, drink, fall, drown, get stuck. He brandished his black gizmo for sucking them out, I guess expecting us to be impressed.

"Wonder about diseases," Byron said to the squirrel, and went inside for a book with the answer.

Dad said if we're talking drowning then why the blood and scrapes.

"Prolly thrashed around a bit," Darren said, "not unusual."

Now or never I saw dad think before he fired the guy. It took Darren a long ten minutes to pack up his crap as we figured out dinner. Mom asked if we wanted barbecued cow and suggested dad would be happy to cook.

Ate out on the deck, slapping ourselves from mosquitoes. The pool quietly hummed and stuttered—there was the factory for you. Byron mentioned getting neighbors to sign a waiver: any of their dumb kids could wander over and . . . whatever. Mom said we'd put in fences, but the zoning.

"Wouldn't be our fault," Kenzie said.

"On our property it is," I told her.

Byron nodded gravely, steak juice dripping.

"I do have PMS," Kenzie pouted. "Can we have separate birthday parties this year?"

Berkie stole the napkin from my lap and fled.

"How's *The Wiz*, you two?" asked mom.

I said fine and Kenzie said good. She's Toto, so how hard could it be.

"He apologize for hitting you in the face?" dad was keen to know.

"Who?" asked Byron.

"Tinman."

"Ryan never hit him," Kenz practically sang, stabbing the potato she refused to eat.

"What I don't get," said dad, the water purring under his voice, "is why you have a bunch of white kids to do that show."

And there were other things he wanted to say.

◊

We carpooled with Ryan, this total wart. Every other morning, his dad drove him, Kenz and me to rehearsal. Byron got dropped at squash or science camp. The two of them lived nearby in half a McMansion sealed up with pink siding—money ran out, mom says. Their crummy jeep's rear window was missing. On cold dewy mornings in the way-back, you felt it. Ryan's dad would blow through town at seventy, telling stories about Iraq or German rollercoasters he'd ridden drunk. American coasters, he assured us, were choking on buttloads of German dust.

"Can we turn on the radio?" Kenzie never gave up asking.

Ryan was even worse than his dad, a rotted-broccoli-smelling ass who blinked too hard. *Squeezed* his eyes shut. Dad couldn't remember his name but called him Tinman, which worked, and made us acknowledge his existence: "Meanwhile, what's up with the Tinman?"

One morning Ryan threw himself into the backseat and breathlessly asked if a blue jay had flown down our chimney, too.

"What," I said, dropping the quarter I'd had walking over my knuckles.

"I heard this flapping when I was on the computer last night, and I went in the den and a blue jay was in the fireplace soot jumping around, like, panicking."

I wondered whether Ryan was retarded.

"Why would that happen to us just cause it happened to you?" Byron asked. Ryan burrowed giggling into his shoulder. Byron pressed his racquet's face to his own. "Kenzie should have to sit in the middle."

"We don't even *have* a chimney," Kenz said, squirming as boys struggled and smushed her against the door.

"Just the hook for Tinman's story," said dad. "Lighten up, Mack."

"Tell By to lighten up."

"Byron, lighten up."

"Had to keep Schmoozer—that's the white cat with spots—we had to keep him away," Ryan went, trying to make Byron punch himself. "Sometimes he brings us a dead mouse or bird like they're presents."

"Ew," said Kenz, "Glad Berkie doesn't do that." She asked if we could turn on the radio. Byron leaned forward, elbowing Ryan in the chest, and dialed to dad's classics station. I reached under the chair for my quarter, touched slime, and kept trying.

◊

Mom spent her vacation talking shit about the guest columnist. She'd mutter acronyms, WTO, J18, G8 . . . said she'd better get the Seattle gig come November. I was up early one Saturday to try a pushup routine and found Kenz on the front porch, peeling off the op-eds. I snuck up behind and scared her bad.

When mom announced she was going to the store for another *Times* since delivery personnel were swiping harebrained opinion where they find it, I said I'd come, but I'm no tattle. Just needed a reason to move, to go anywhere: the bubbling hot tub was too relaxing. I slipped over the divide into the colder pool, shocking my skin awake.

When I came to the driveway, the Runt was leaning against the Explorer with her arms folded, mom cycling through a dozen keys to find the right one.

You promised, Mack mouthed before turning to bare fixed teeth at mom. She asked if we could get pet rabbits, a boy and a girl. Mom opened the car with the key, not the button, and said there were too many rabbits in the world as is.

Inside, the dog went nuts.

Found her standing in the den, barking right in Byron's face, Byron doing sit-ups in a tank top, watching *Alfred Hitchcock Presents* like he didn't notice.

Brushing dark dog hair off jagged mini-muscles as he folded up. Berkie glanced over a shoulder and thumped her tail against my shin when she saw the harness.

I led her out back. Forgot to kill the Jacuzzi bubbles, so I hit the switch on the side of the waterfall. Buzzing quit, but the pool lights came on, weak in the daytime, a ring of drowned baby suns. Berkie curled up next to the water.

◈

When we got back, Dad called me into the office. Said I touched the pool controls. Aren't you supposed to? He called me Smartass and asked where we'd been.

"They don't need your help shopping . . . hang out with girls enough already."

"They asked me."

"You're old for it."

"Kenzie went."

He was *curious* what we'd covered in health class. Everything, I thought.

"Some people are late bloomers, and some are not," he said. "Everybody's different. You know?" I had to zone out as the talk went on—there was bad calm in it.

"Respect girls and don't get one pregnant," I heard.

In the fax tray were papers that had gone through. Top one had Darren's name and number. A picture of his truck.

"Anything you want to tell me?" dad went. "You know I love you no matter what."

Makes me wonder what awful shit he thinks I do.

Snuck out that night. Everyone went to Ryan's basement cause his dad was Never There, Didn't Care. More people than last time, most from the play. Schmoozer went around trying to get attention. Wanted to pet him, but allergies. Ryan drank two beers and interrupted my quarter tricks to announce that someone's parents weren't divorced.

You're the oooonly one, he crooned.

I drank some more but didn't feel it.

What was with this girl? I'd talked to her only once at rehearsal . . . she shoved me into the bathroom like she'd had it all planned out and made me take my clothes off. Blew me cause she wanted to. First I gently tried to stop it, then I watched the doorknob and worried. Was I allowed to touch her tits during? I didn't, to be safe. Then she put my hands there and I was so pissed at myself for not. A knocking started, the doorknob rattled and I probably said *No.* Couldn't decide what to do at the end, so I stopped thinking, which made the end come sooner.

I crept back over our lawn, the grass rustling louder than fucking World War II. Lifted the second-to-last flagstone on the front path and felt out our spare key in the dirt. Found the front door. Missed the lock and dropped the key. Bending over was like: maybe I'll puke.

Darren's pickup was across the street.

Parked. I stared. Must have been there a while. Glowing white in the dark. Shadows sliced across letters on the side, hiding everything but MENACE. I re-read MAINTENANCE.

I blinked and was walking over without a plan.

The truck coughed dryly and sped away with its headlights still off.

Down the street, another ignition caught, and a van rolled past, following Darren at a distance.

Felt better.

The house was asleep but I couldn't close my eyes. In the den I rewound Byron's video. Maybe cause of the beers I couldn't follow the story—something about blackmail—and the lamp next to me kept flickering. Burnt my fingers trying to screw the lightbulb tighter. Hitchcock said if anyone from the year 2000 was watching, they ought to send him a letter about life in the future.

Overhead there were two thuds like heavy luggage dropping, and Berkie lost it outside. Glass broke. Dad said something, but "fucking" and "baby" was all I caught. "Grow up," mom's clear voice sang, like Mackenzie's. "He's not out for revenge." Their bedroom door slammed too hard to close—I heard it swing back. Dad asking. Mom: "Take it, then."

Another slam, and it stuck this time.

I remembered. Snapped the light off and rolled under the couch.

Dad's feet slapped across the wood. He turned off the static, mumbling, "Byron." His bathing suit fell close to my face and he picked it up and walked on, popping a beer in the kitchen. The sliding backdoor scraped. Flickering light was still there, in waves on the floor. I crawled over and squatted next to the bamboo plant by the open glass door where central air wrestled with gross heat.

It was the pool lights that were spazzing. They briefly shot on full. Saw dad at the control panel across the water, jabbing with a knuckle. He stopped to change out of his boxers and I looked away just in time, above the stammering blue. He gave the panel a good kick and colors turned off. Waterfall hiccupped once.

A splash. Berkie on the far side, zipping back and forth on her cable, growling at dad as he cut white wake in the dark. She hated the idea of swimming itself. Black fur shining in the moonlight—an inkblot running along the rim of an inkwell. Eventually the inkblot broke from its rut and went off into hanging black shapes.

Dad swam full laps before taking air. I tried to hold my breath as long.

There was a wobbly screech, the finale of Kenzie's orthodontist nightmare, maybe, and dad paused for a minute. He stood in the shallow end, waiting for more.

The baby suns blazed suddenly, circling him, bubbles madly foaming in the hot tub. His head flung moondrops in every direction.

Electricity fell away again.

Then Byron's true factory noise in total blindness, a swallowing torrent of air like jet engines. Something touched the edge of the wind and was taken up; it caught against a wall of steel, killed the storm with an echoless clang.

And there, with my sight weak and slowly rebooting, was dad crashing through a churned oil that used to divide into water and night, a creature all teeth and hair and fingers trying to be born, to wake evolved out of streaming ooze, to find an edge and pull itself up.

◊

Next morning I said I was too sick for rehearsal and lay awake, hard white daytime creeping over my bed. Took the Victoria's Secret catalog out of my desk but couldn't get things going. Models stared at you like they were disappointed. I was sick of my CDs too—annoying little kid music. A buzzing roar turned out to be the landscapers' mower, and from the window I watched them sweat through the afternoon.

Kenzie's crying came through the vents. Realized I'd finally fallen asleep.

Stayed at the top of the stairs, asking if it was safe to come down.

"Come in here if you want to talk," mom went.

In the kitchen I found her and Kenzie, folder of death threats between them on the counter. Through the sliding door sat the pool, wet patches on its cover sparkling with sunset.

"Why do you keep them?" Kenzie demanded.

"So sensitive," mom went, chopping up onions.

"If any of them *do* kill mom," Byron yelled from the bathroom, "we'll have a good case for premeditated." The toilet flushed way loud.

"Mack, honey, these people are losers. I'm not the one outsourcing."

"Murders by assembly line workers are up," Byron quoted as he came out waving dad's piece in *Time*.

"Stop!" Kenzie cried. Mom dumped the onions in a pan and groaned.

"Stop saying 'stop,' " she went. "You may no longer say 'stop.' "

"Is there a personal hate letter from Darren?" Byron asked. He picked up mom's reminder notepad and tapped his lips with a pen.

"That you'll have to ask your father," mom said.

Kenzie turned to me and mentioned that after rehearsal a girl was asking for me. Maybe one of the dancers. I had to know which, but naturally she couldn't remember the name, only what color nail polish.

"I told her not to bother since you have no personality."

Nobody replied, but Byron smirked the right way, never even looked up from his writing. We waited until mom left before plucking Mack from the stool and hefting her to the backyard, stretched and swinging like a hammock between us.

"This is why no one likes you!" she screeched. Byron lifted a few cicada skins from the trees that separate our yard from the Petruzellis' and hung them by their barbs in Mack's hair while she bellowed and tried to spin out of my headlock.

"Tell us to stop," Byron said.

"Ew," she spat, "your breath is nasty."

I asked, did somebody have a bad dream last night? Who's a baby? Who let their imagination get away with them?

Dad came out back carrying a long metal pole with hook and net attachments and muttered mom better not've called Darren already. What to say to that. We dropped Kenz, who ran off. Dad toed a spot on the lawn where the grass was yellow, jammed the hook extension on. Flipped up a corner of the pool cover and kneeled over the gaping filter duct, feeding the pole in from above. There was nothing on the hook when it came out. We waited, and a bloodslick cruised into view.

"Yup," dad said. He pushed the pole back in, scraping, tongue bent in the corner of his mouth. Handfuls of grass and dirt floated free. Then a slashed rabbit. He swapped the hook for the net and fished it out, told Byron to get a garbage bag.

"How'd you know?" he asked.

"Didn't," said dad. "Rabbit screams sound like a kid's."

Byron and I followed him around to the driveway to see how you disposed of dead animals. The trash cans were knocked over, shredded cereal boxes and string cheese wrappers everywhere.

Raccoons, dad said, *again.*

We helped cleaned it up. The rabbit went in with the rest of the garbage. The garbage went out to the street for collection.

◊

Had to dress up for a muscular dystrophy dinner. Berkie kept tugging Byron's black socks off his feet. Mom reminded us that we had long ago promised to walk a dog if we got one. Dad added that responsibility is a thing we might try.

"Poor girl was out all night," he informed us.

"Always sleeps in my room," Kenzie went, using up mom's lipstick, adjusting ransacked jewelry. "She likes to protect me." So, were we going to tell her that wasn't true? I turned to do Byron's tie, but he'd gotten it.

"Don't lose my earrings," mom said. "Remember the AIDS banquet." Kenzie handed the silver tube back, snapping her compact shut in my face.

"Nobody felt worse about that than me."

As we walked out I tore the top sheet off mom's notepad and shoved it in my blazer pocket. Soon as I could, I ducked out of the Hilton ballroom and sat in a stall in a freezing men's room that smelled like someone was shitting cologne, smoothed it out and read.

Dear Mr. Hitchcock—

Still a few months until the year 2000, but trust me, it'll be too much.

I came back to him and Kenzie guffawing over each other as the grown-ups tried to take a picture on stage. Byron filled me in:

"Mom was threatening to adopt one of the muscular dystrophy kids."

"If we didn't behave!" gasped Kenzie. "How bout a deformed baby brother?"

The photographer waved for the sides to squeeze in.

"I reminded her they already had parents," went Byron.

"Wouldn't stand a chance against us," I said. Found a quarter in my pocket and bounced it into Kenzie's half-full water glass.

"Sharing with you two is bad enough," she admitted.

"Blame science," said Byron. "Works too well."

"I want a kid . . ." I prompted.

"Here's three!" we shouted together.

◊

Next rehearsal, same old. You Can't Win stopped right as we got to the box-step that needed work. The crows groaned.

"Scarecrow's got to have more soul," Mr. Dunbar said, a bald spot bouncing behind the upright piano. "Dance with *soul*." Kenzie cracked up in the wing. "Have you watched the original?" Dunbar asked for the millionth time.

"Hey Brainless," Kenzie called when I came backstage. "Hey Bitch," I went. "Not funny," she pouted. Ryan popped out from behind a flat with city skyline painted on and invited us to a party. When Kenz got away he said she'd bring other girls, right? Asked if Byron would come too. Told him no one wanted that.

The dancers passed through in a whispering knot. None were wearing pink nail polish.

At home dad said to hold off on the pool. He fetched the pole, did the routine and freed a raccoon with its throat inside out. Screwed open a valve next to the waterfall and dumped powder in, told us to wait another half hour. We sat pulling grass up till a killer skunk smell made us run inside.

Figured I might as well practice that Mozart. Turned out I still sucked. From the kitchen I heard mom say, "Darren? It . . . yeah." Then dad, stomping up from the basement. "Give me." A violent crash in the glass recycling. Phone clattering on linoleum. "No, I do not need your help," dad said—into the phone, I think. "I know what you did."

Weak heartbeats. Byron hitting a squash ball against the outside of the house, regular as a metronome. I started to play in time.

"Since then it's been clockwork." dad went. "Controls are glitched. And there's no reason you can think of."

Mom yelled for me to stop playing, then asked nicely if I could get a new bottle from the downstairs fridge. I played louder, with more mistakes.

"You think I won't do something about your behavior?" dad said.

Mom asked if I'd heard her.

"Come in here if you want to talk," I offered.

"Say it's normal again," dad went. "See what happens."

A damp hand landed on my shoulder. Made me play worse. Moved to my cheek. You could feel her swaying to the music.

"It's beautiful," she said. "What is it?"

"Mozart Fantasy in C Minor."

"You have no idea, do you," dad said.

"Play me something," she went. Her fingers found my neck. "You never play."

"I'm trying."

The phone slammed down.

"Play something and sing with it."

"No," I said.

"It's so easy to make me happy, and no one wants to." She wrapped me from behind and kissed the top of my head.

"Got that out of your system?" mom said, joining dad in the kitchen. He said he was sorry, then talked softly. Mom snorted.

"We'll see," she laughed.

I got up and peered around the corner. Dad was kissing her against the wall.

Even with bug candles we got eaten at dinner. Fireflies were pulsing in force. Pool lights winked out. Minutes later they started blinking.

"Great corn," mom mentioned.

"Ready," said Byron.

"Ready," mimicked Kenz.

"That's what the pool is flashing."

"Stop," I said.

"How come he gets to say it," Kenzie whined, "and *I* get in trouble."

"All in the delivery," dad went.

"Did you call someone about the possums under the porch?" mom asked.

"In Morse code," said Byron, "it's ready for sure."

"You all hate me," Kenz said.

And the hot tub bubbled expectantly.

◊

Dad plumbed the pool filter for dead things daily. Once it was a blue jay and crow together, which mom said was good news for her flowers. "But those deer've been wreaking havoc on the garden, too." Dad taught us his method for yanking the animals out. Just a regular chore. When I slept through the factory noise, it got into dreams as a tornado that danced across my tongue. We once pried a skunk out of the chute. Doesn't stink when it's dead, I noted. Byron shook his head.

"Pool's always trying new things," he said.

"Darren's doing it," I said. "Don't you know anything?"

"Darren," Byron smiled, "*must* have better things to do."

We got dad when something was wedged too tight. He couldn't work it loose either, searched the yellow pages for a new pool guy to help him extract a white-dotted fawn. Unballed on the grass, you could see gashes like a lion had brought it down, the flattened fur standing as it dried. Berkie trotted over and put her nose against its belly. Tried to nudge it back towards the pool, pushed and whimpered, and that's still the saddest thing I've seen.

◊

She ran away the next day. Sort of. Sometimes you'd pick out her jangling choke chain in all the night sounds. But it would fade into gurgling water or dissolve under cicada drones.

Can't remember when I closed the piano for good and noticed the jangle closer than usual. Brightness rung across the patio, dimming in the yard. I slid the door open and heard the chain out on the grass like a pocket full of quarters, this rhythmic panting. We hadn't blown out the bug candles or new tiki torches, and beyond them glowed the yellow-black curve of Berkie's back as she stooped to dig. Her head snapped up once—I was sure I'd been caught—but she bowed again, picking up a ragged hank of fur that dripped gold. She laid the creature belly-up in its grave and stretched her front legs to sort of bow before the gift.

A pencil-thin pink tail flicked out in the stillness, the possum nearly dead or done bluffing. Berkie reared back, not expecting it: her snarls bled into the savage hum, spun into the factory's killing note and quickened blue. My heart twisted backwards, trying to look away.

Kenzie put up lost dog signs, but we had no picture to go with. Main difference was the quiet. Still that coat of blue-black hairs on everything.

◊

On Monday, Ryan's dad was more spaced than usual, chanting softly to turn approaching red lights green, running them if it didn't work. Kenz told us the Navy was hunting for pieces of JFK Jr.'s plane.

"Ever played Cloud Nine?" Ryan asked.

"Don't you *care?*" Kenzie went.

"What do you do?" I asked from the way-back, since I definitely did not care. Ryan unbuckled himself and turned to face Byron.

"Take a deep breath and hold it," he instructed. Byron was bored enough to play along. Ryan waited, lunged and tried to crush him in a bear hug. Byron got a hand free and put it to Ryan's jaw, pushing him into Kenzie. She screamed. Ryan's dad spun and was on the point of saying something when a bone-ringing crunch threw us ahead.

Ryan was out cold, blood on his ear. In my gut the crash hadn't ended, so how was a woman already at his dad's window, screaming herself hoarse as he put his head to the wheel and let the horn blare?

POLLUTO.

That Friday, he called to weasel out of his turn. Mom picked up the phone at breakfast and shook her head with true pity, walked into the bathroom to relay the flake-out.

"That fucking *loser!*" dad roared from the shower. He'd forgotten the new phone was cordless—Mom was holding it. Ryan's dad heard.

"Why can't he drive?" Mackenzie asked after the fight, lacing the guest columnist's picture with graffiti from mom's red pen. "We should kick him out of the carpool anyhow."

Dad could barely finish his sentence.

"He forgot . . . he had to get married . . . *today* . . . in *Japan.*"

"Should've mail-ordered," chimed mom from the study.

We had to laugh that night: dad told us *Time* was sending him to Tokyo to cover the ANA Flight 61 story. Byron told him to have fun at the wedding.

He faxed us a note the next day with details: this psycho had popped a ton of antidepressants, stabbed the captain, and driven the plane crazy low, planning to fly under the Rainbow Bridge. *Skyjacking, then, can be as much joyride as message,* he ended up writing in the article, which made sense to me.

Ryan's blowout was that night. Guess he didn't clinch Best Man. I was supposed to meet Kenzie out back after mom went to bed. Came near the waterfall and saw the shape of a boy with her, caving in the pool cover with his foot. I coughed to interrupt them, but it was only Byron.

"Surprise," he said.

At Ryan's I found the girl who'd picked me out before. She led me to a door we couldn't open, then a bedroom. Shoved me into a mirror that cracked under my back. Said I thought I was better than everybody, that's why I never talked. I said I was just shy. She grabbed everything in a pink-nailed fist and said she liked it in her mouth because then she had the power. I didn't like thinking about that. Or the loose pieces of mirror that would fall if I stepped away.

"Try," she said. "You won't break me."

◊

45

There was no reason for me to give Kenzie shit about drinking, and she left with a beer before it got nasty. Ryan came into the kitchen and told me Byron was here like I didn't know. Would've been great to kick his teeth in.

"Thought triplets got along famously," he said.

"That's twins," I told him.

We looked into the other room and saw a new boy touching Byron's hair. He said something and raised an eyebrow. Byron turned to look at us and laughed. Ryan begged me to help with wide, wide eyes.

I wandered the unfinished parts of the house. Suffocating paint smell. Upstairs, black ragged holes where light switches would go. Something flashed in moonlight and I took a step towards it, calling, "Schmoozer?"

The floor wasn't there, only a softness of nothing and cool rush, falling forever before the bottom slammed up beneath me. I inhaled sawdust. My ribs were bent, exploded. I reached out . . . my fingertips curling over a curved saw blade . . . skeleton buzzing in distant pain. Surely part of my body was gone. Standing took a few tries. I was wet with beer and the sawdust stuck to it. I groped around the sleeping equipment, led myself by bundled wires back to where everything dropped out, the doorframe of the unfinished room. The cliff was only a foot or two high. A line from Orange Club swim lessons sifted through the haze: *you can drown in just an inch of water.*

Limping out of the house alone when I heard a smack and strangled cry from the second floor. The way Byron rushed down the stairs, I knew Ryan'd made his move. I opened the front door and rubbed my loose face, holding an arm out. After you. He grunted and strode out.

We shuffled across the neighbors' backyards and into ours, saying nothing. Sent an animal scuttling through mom's hydrangeas and towards the street.

"Want to play Cloud Nine?" I said, just to be weird, and hug-tackled Byron. He tried to keep walking with me strapped to his torso, dead serious, and was strong enough. But the harder I squeezed, the more he smiled. He finally went limp on purpose and we collapsed, drunk, laughing, rolling in wet grass. Byron rested a minute on his back, eyebrows pressed downward. He reached under himself and pulled out Darren's visor.

◊

Dad didn't make it back to the country in time for the play, which I didn't mind. The four of us went out to Sul Fiume—Kenzie's favorite for the Baccalà Fritte—and we even got a table with a view of the river. Mom said our show was "so fresh" and that I was funniest. When the food took longer than normal, Byron pointed to a guy wading with a rod in the shallows outside.

"Can't eat 'til he catches Mack's fish," he said, and we laughed, Kenzie too. Even Mom stopped chewing her nails to smile. I didn't try to make a joke after that.

The guy reeled in a clean hook again. He cast.

Dad called that night and said he was homesick, sounded like he meant it.

◊

Day before high school started, Byron and I had to pull the tarp back over the pool. A storm had left half the pool exposed. Dad said to anchor it with rocks this time. Byron went hunting for big enough ones while I dragged the plastic sheeting into place. Kenzie was sunning with her discman in the Adirondack.

Sat with my feet in the water, waiting for Byron. Shouldn't have been so warm: we'd shut off the heat weeks ago, when we'd all quit swimming. Red rings collecting around my ankles. I got on my stomach and let my head hang over the edge.

Looking into the filter's tunnel, I couldn't see the swinging metal flap at the end. The space was filled with lumpy darkness. Byron tapped me on the shoulder and held out the pole. I took it and fished around inside, jabbing the lumps. The hook didn't go through but caught something hard. I wobbled it loose. Grass and pink threads of flesh stuck to the metal. By now Kenzie was standing over me, her face weirdly stretched. I looked down the tunnel again and a small white crescent hovered in black. A smile floating upside down.

47

When they unfolded Darren from his fetal knot, I could see from the patio a hole in the neck where I must've hooked him, Xs of grassblades plastered to pruny skin, his dozen extra joints. A bad mix of drugs in his system, they said. Was in the neighborhood, knew the house, stupidly decided to swim. Maybe drawn towards the lights. Got stuck, struggled. Not that complicated. It's ugly, improbable, but it happens.

"Anybody wants to confess to cramming him in there, now's the time," a detective said on his way out. "No? Makes my life easier."

Kenzie freaked that Darren had been prowling around.

Mom was sick, insisted we pave over the pool, "erase it." Dad shrugged. He was in no special rush.

Byron assured me Morse code was to blame.

And you could tell he was laughing inside.

THE END

NINE DAYS: THE STONE BOY'S LAMENT

KURT KIRCHMEIER

They sculpted me from stone and placed me high upon a ledge below the spire, a gargoyle in the form of a child, a symbolic reminder for those who'd forgotten whence magic came.

Beneath me stood the thaumaturgists' library, a two-storied affair that housed the work of a thousand mage-scholars, each with a voice and a legacy of words.

Magic, they all agreed, sprang from the minds of children. Through innocence and imagination, impossibility found purchase in the world. Without the young, there would be no spells, no words to commit to paper.

But words are like symbols, subject to misinterpretation, misrepresentation. Such was the reason I parted my stone lips and sucked air. Magic had been abused, innocence corrupted for war and greed and vanity.

On the first day I merely wandered, absorbing the world's vibrations like a sponge, looking for cracks in the foundation, rifts of silence in the song. In the city there were many, in the forests just a few; I found peace there, in the trees, a heartbeat akin to my own, and though I longed to lay down and rest my head on the moss for eternity, to become one with the birds and the flowers, the mosquitoes and the pines, my journey had only just begun.

To the city I returned.

On the second day I preached, though not in the manner of my elders. I smiled at those I conversed with, unaware that my elementary words fell on unconcerned ears.

"Not fair," I said, "not right." I used words like "mean" and "bad" and sometimes "sad."

On the third day I wondered why no one had listened. Walking through labyrinthine alleyways, I found evidence of both spells misused and spells that should've been used but weren't.

At midday I saw a dog get kicked so hard that something broke inside it. With a curse of dismissal, its owner abandoned it to the cobblestones. It lay for a long while whining and crying, waiting for a healing spell that would never come. I'd have provided one myself, but magic wasn't yet mine to use; I was a child only, a catalyst.

"Mister?" I begged a passerby. "Hey, Mister, won't you spare some magic for this little dog?" But the owner returned and shooed me away, said the mutt had it coming and that I'd have it coming too unless I scrammed. And so I did, far enough to remain unseen, near enough to still hear the whimpering. I snuck back to the dog's side later on, and silenced it in the only way I could think to do so: with a large rock.

On the fourth day I planted a cross and watered it with tears.

On the fifth day I resumed my task in earnest, the fate of the dog a cornerstone for my resolve. Late afternoon I chanced upon a soup kitchen, and found within the hands of generosity, but nary a spell to go with them.

As I shuffled between rows of rickety tables and rickety benches I wondered at the lack of magic, for surely there were catalysts aplenty; then my eyes connected with those of a rickety child, and instantly I knew. They'd aged beyond their skins, these many lads and lasses—children on the outside, shattered on the in. Though imagination remained, of innocence there was none. A catalyst halved is no catalyst at all.

"More?" said a girl with pigtails. But the soup bowl was empty, on the bread pans only crumbs.

"Take from me," I said to the lady with the ladle. "Take magic for my fellow boys and girls. Make soup and bread and pudding."

She graced me with a butter-melting smile, dimples like raisins in her cheeks. "If I could, child, I would, but I'm a peasant, you see, poor and illiterate. Magic is for the privileged."

I regarded the still-hungry girl, and thought to myself: not fair, not right.

On the sixth day I returned to the library and borrowed new words to replace those that'd already failed me. "Mean" became "unjust" and "bad" became "oppressive." In place of "sad" I chose "despairing."

On the seventh day I preached a second time, but still they wouldn't listen; still they didn't hear. They smiled at my adult posturing, shared laughter at my verbosity.

"Well now," they said, "aren't you just the cutest little politician!" They pinched my cheek for good measure.

On the eighth day I lamented my failings, then wondered if an audience of my peers might better receive my ramblings. And so back to the kitchen I went to regale the hungry youngsters with the content of my days.

I spoke of the fallen dog, spoke of necessary change, and though they listened intent on my words, they dispersed as if they hadn't heard me at all.

Rather than plead with their elders, individual voices made strong by numbers, they instead clenched their fists and rose as an angry mob.

To the house of the martyred dog they marched, whereupon they struck matches and set the place afire.

Smoke poured from the open windows, but the owner must've been sleeping, for his exit was much belated. His clothes were covered in flames, his hair a ravenous torch. Soon he lay dead on the cobblestones, in the exact spot his dog had been.

I wept as the match-strikers cheered, for I'd forgotten that words were like symbols, subject to misinterpretation, misrepresentation. But words were all I had; empty morsels in the mouth of this stone-boy come to life.

On the ninth day I set about committing my actions to paper, immortalizing the loss of my innocence for posterity. Perhaps in time, as this parchment yellows and cracks with age, my words will sharpen, and be imbued with the veracity I seek. Perhaps a wise man will read them and wield them as his own, but in a way that steals not from the young in heart or mind.

In the meantime, they can find me atop the library, a symbol returned to stone, impaled upon the spire.

THE END

MUD WRESTLING IN A DISTANT LAND

MARSHALL PAYNE

You know how to wrestle, don't you?" the future-man asked Tom Tum. "Same damn thing, just get down in the mud-pit and do it!"

Tom looked around at the bizarre world the four of them had just materialized in, a far cry from his 1930s Hollywood. A cockfight of sorts, but this one featuring Tom and his three midget castmates. Darren T. and Minutia Floyd were best known from *The Wizard of Oz*, while Tom and Muscular Marty were minor actors of all-midget Westerns.

"Now get to it, you fucking midget!" the future-man cried.

Dressed only in spa robes, the four full-sized men peered down deviously. "Quite fine of you to feature midgets this time, Bartharon," said the corpulent man in the red robe. Around the huge room, movie screens of a fashion flickered twisted images.

"Yes, but where did you get them?" asked the purple-robed man with huge jowls. "I thought midgets were gengineered out long ago."

"They were," said Bartharon. "This is the new temporal entertainment I was telling you about. I plucked these from the 20th century."

Resounding *ahhs* from the other two, but a puzzled look from the fourth who said, "Aren't there governors to this new technology?"

"Yes, there are," said Bartharon. "But I overrode the parameters. Typically they're supposed to fade back after a few hours, but where's the fun in that?"

Laughter from the deviant future-folk.

"Didn't you hear me, midget?" Bartharon hollered. "You're mine and I've got more than a few creds riding on you. Get after it! Make Papa proud." He chuckled mirthlessly.

Tom was paired against Minutia Floyd, which was a small relief. Not only was Muscular Marty a dear friend, but he was a stout midget and Tom didn't relish being bested by him. Soon Tom and Floyd were hard at it, wallowing in the muck within the ring. But Minutia Floyd was a tough little fellow, possessing more brawn than his tiny size might indicate.

The four future-men catcalled raucously as the two went at it. But soon they grew bored and forced Darren T. and Muscular Marty into the ring to join them.

"Tom," Muscular Marty grunted as he had Darren T. in a headlock. "Where is this place? Where *are* we?"

But Tom didn't answer, as he had none.

After about forty-five minutes of the most strenuous exertion Tom had ever endured, the match was called to a halt.

"Now the real pleasure begins," Bartharon said to his companions. Then: "Okay, small men. Everyone 'out of the pool.'"

The others chortled.

POLLUTO.

As Tom looked up, he saw that each man held a hangman's noose in one hand, chalice of ale in the other. The images around the room still flickered, and Tom realized they only slightly resembled his cherished silver screen from his own time. Three-D, they were, with lewd figures engaging in . . .

As Tom climbed from the mud-pit, he saw the bulge beneath Bartharon's robe and knew what the men had in mind.

THE END

LIFE'S NECESSITIES

DEBORAH WALKER

It was like living in prison; virtually everything she needed was denied her.

"I need a new coat for school," Ayesha said. She had carefully chosen her moment. Her mother appeared to be in a good mood.

"I bought you a new coat last week." Her mother's voice was threaded with irritation. Apparently, Ayesha had misjudged her mother's mood, but she persisted.

Ayesha took off her coat and slapped it on the table amongst the remains of breakfast. The half empty cups of coffee rattled. "Just look at this," she gestured to the coat with an abrupt movement of her hand.

Apart from a few crumbs of breakfast bread, the coat looked immaculate.

"What's wrong with the coat, Ayesha?" Her mother's voice had changed now. It contained the sound of weariness, an awareness of the argument that shimmered in the air. There was always a disagreement waiting to be pulled into existence through the economies of their unchanging attitudes. These disagreements were a regular part of the daughter-mother communications. In fact, for the last six months, they were the only daughter-mother communications.

But Ayesha was not discouraged. She had the optimism of youth on her side. She believed that she could change her mother's opinions by the force of her reasonable arguments. "I've been wearing that coat all week. I need a new one."

"Not on my card."

"But, Mum, my friends will laugh at me if I wear this coat again."

"No 'buts,' and that's the end of it. Have you considered that your friends aren't really friends if they only care about your clothes?"

Ayesha dragged the coat off the breakfast table. The red fur, intermingled with tiny glowing lights, looked so dated. She remembered how desperate she'd been to acquire it a week ago, how much her friends had admired it. But that was then, and this was now. The coat was old now. As she gathered the warm, red fur into her arms, she noticed that it was smeared with butter. What did it matter if it was stained? She'd be a laughing stock anyway.

"Thanks a lot, Mother. And please don't talk about my friends. You don't know anything about them." Her mother! What did she know? There had been no supermarkets when she was young. She didn't understand. Still, her mother's insidious words crawled into Ayesha's mind. Her friends, Michaela, Peppy and the rest, would they still like her if she wasn't able to get the latest outfits? What about Zach? What would he think? Ayesha didn't know the answers to those questions, and she didn't want to find out.

She put on the soiled coat. Wearing something so old made her feel dirty.

Please, let them not notice. Please, let them not notice, she prayed to an unfamiliar god. *Let me get away with it for a few more days.*

"I'm going to school."

"Look, Ayesha, I'll see what I can do next week. It is difficult though. I don't want to get too much debt onto my card. Maybe if I can get a few hours of work, I can offset some of the credit, but there's so little work available for ordinary people nowadays. The automatons are taking all the work, you know . . . "

"Yes, do whatever you want. Don't worry about me. I'm only your daughter," said Ayesha. Predictably, she slammed the door on her way out to school.

◊

Ayesha sat with her best friend in the school cafeteria. Michaela had her own supermarket card. It was so unfair. Ayesha, as the youngest girl in her class, was the only one who didn't have her own card. Who made these arbitrary rules anyway?

Seated together the two girls made a contrasting pair. Ayesha looked ordinary, a slim frame, brown eyes and hair all within the standard range. But Michaela, with her access to the supermarket's body-morph section, looked unusual. She had chosen a dappled pattern to her skin, and her eyes were stretched to give her an extended vision. Animal variations were very popular this month.

As soon as I turn fifteen, I'm going to look extraordinary too, thought Ayesha. *But how can I stand out? You can only buy what's on offer*. Ayesha looked around; probably fifty percent of the people in this cafeteria looked extraordinary. At what point does the strange become commonplace?

"What do you think about the new Feelers in the supermarket?" asked Michaela.

"The shoes?"

"Yep, do you like them?"

Ayesha had to be careful, sometimes Michaela tricked her, led her into saying things.

So instead of answering, Ayesha said, "How much have you got on your card, Michaela?"

"Two years, I think."

Two years in two months. Wow. How could Ayesha ever catch up?

"That's a lot," said Ayesha. "Aren't you worried?" The thought just slipped out.

"When you're dead, you're dead," said Michaela, raising her lacquered fingernails to her face. The nails flickered with tiny images.

"These are real life images of the Viper Colony," said Michaela, holding out her hand so that Ayesha could admire them. "Look, you can almost make out the prisoners' expressions if you look close enough."

"Wow, that's nasty. They must have been really expensive."

"They cost me two months," said Michaela.

Ayesha envied Michaela's wild spending. It must be wonderful to buy whatever you wanted. Well, in a few more months, Ayesha would outspend them all.

"Will you look at that," said Michaela, breaking into Ayesha's daydreams of uncontrollable acquisitions. She pointed an image-lacquered nail to a group sitting on the outskirts of the cafeteria.

"Self-servicers," said Ayesha, looking over at a group of teenagers dressed in home-spun cloth and rough hand-knitted jumpers.

"How can they bear to come to school like that?"

"I hear that they don't even have automatons in their own homes."

"What? Who does all the housework?"

58

"They do it themselves, I guess. In between weaving their own clothes." The girls laughed.

"Oooh, that's funny. Still, I suppose they have to do what their parents make them do," said Ayesha. "It's not really their fault."

Michaela pointed to at a girl with straight blonde hair. It just hung there, it wasn't styled or anything. "I happen to know that Mistral has her own card. That outfit is her own choice." Michaela waved to Mistral, who ignored her. "They try to live without the supermarket. What losers."

"It's tragic," agreed Ayesha. A thought surfaced within her, something that was constantly on her mind. She said, casually, "By the way, have you seen Zach today?"

"No, not today. But did I tell you that he said 'hello' to me in P.E., yesterday?"

"Yep, you mentioned it." Loyalty and jealousy fought for a moment within Ayesha. Then she said, "I bet he noticed you new body-mods. They're fab."

"Thanks, babes. I love your coat, by the way. I've always liked it. But shall we go to the supermarket after school to check out the latest acquisitions?"

The girls left the table. An automaton came over and began clearing away their discarded meal.

◊

The next day found Ayesha in her mother's bedroom, moving the clothes and books littering the bedroom floor, and carefully replacing them in their original positions. She was looking for her mother's card. It was surprising that someone who was so careful with her credit often left her card lying around the house.

The compulsion to spend was strong in Ayesha. She had to do something. She could feel her status slipping at school. She yearned to be part of the accepted crowd. Ayesha and Michaela ran at the periphery of the most popular group at school. Sometimes they were invited to parties; sometimes they were allowed to share the jokes. But their status was precarious. They couldn't quite penetrate into the heart of coolness. But Michaela, with her new modifications, was rising in the ranks. Soon Ayesha would be left behind, one of the many admirers who stood on the margins admiring the glory of the inner core.

Sure, she could join one of the other groups, maybe even head one. But she wanted to be part of Zach's group, Zach with the liquid wit and the harsh smile, shocking Zach with his snide comments in class and his anger bubbling within the surface of him—hot to touch. If only Ayesha could get close to him.

Ah, she had it. Her mother's life card glittered in her fingers. Ayesha could spend a day or two, and her mother wouldn't notice. Her mother only glanced at her supermarket statements; she preferred not to know the balance of her account.

And Ayesha would buy her something really special, really expensive. When she had her own card, she would pay her mother back.

Ayesha dressed in her best clothes. The clothes felt great, apart from the dreadful coat, of course. She even felt a small a stab of remorse when she realised that she was wearing six months worth of clothing. The debt accumulated so rapidly. But she quickly suppressed her guilt; she needed to do this.

◈

Walking into the supermarket was an altogether different experience when you had a card. She really was a slave to her mother. It was only right that she had taken her mother's card. She deserved it.

Ayesha walked through the marble doors of the supermarket. Since her last visit, yesterday, the supermarket had been re-designed. The supermarket was unselfconscious in its most recent architecture: it was a temple to acquisition. Each supermarket was unique and special—it made the consumers feel special to lavish such wealth on the building, and the building constantly changed. It was an adventure to come here, there was always something new and extraordinary to look at. And, why not? In a palace of dreams you should feel special.

The customary supermarket warning flashed into Ayesha's vision: No Refunds. No Excuses. The letters hung for a moment in the air in front of Ayesha.

As she entered, she saw that the supermarket was very busy. It was always busy in the supermarket—there were a lot of things to buy. Several automatons rushed up to greet her. They had been re-designed as someone's idea of a slave girl. Their metallic limbs glinted out of folds of diaphanous linen, and a band of gold shone around their necks. Jewels sparkled on the wires which connected their metal body to the organic gloop within their heads.

All the automatons were women today, and Ayesha wondered if any of the bodies contained the personalities of men. How would that feel, to be encased not only in the metal shell, but to be trapped inside a body of the wrong sex?

But the automatons didn't feel anything, they weren't real. Or if they did feel something, it was just the echoes of the person that they once were. Still, it was disconcerting to imagine the personality of a man inside these lush, suggestive metallic bodies.

"Go away," said Ayesha as a slave girl tried to press some special coupons into her hand. "I'm not interested."

She wished that they would leave her alone. It was rather off-putting to see the sad creatures, milling around, trying to sell you things. They were spoiling the whole experience for her. This was a special day, the first time she had come to the supermarket alone. She usually came here with her mother, but she had something better than her mother with her today; she had her mother's card.

She walked on through the enormous, vaulted halls. You could spend all day examining the goods and not see one tenth of the items. You had to plan, and have a strategy to get the best shopping experience.

Ayesha decided to focus on shoes. Michaela had said something about Feelers yesterday, and Ayesha was keen to keep up with the latest trends.

She examined the Feelers for an hour. They really were quite innovative, an organic web linked to the pressure centres in your foot. It was able to replicate many walking experiences. She tried them on. Ayesha walked on hot burning sand. Ayesha walked through snow. Ayesha walked on water.

Ayesha was setting the shoes to replicate the "walking on fire experience" when she saw Zack. Heat rushed into her face, she developed an intense interest in a pair of shoes on a high shelf—stretching upwards made her look thinner.

"Hello. Let me get that for you."

"Hello."

"What are you doing?"

"Oh, just browsing," she said as if she was in here on her own all the time. "I'm thinking about buying some shoes, but they're getting awfully expensive aren't they?" There was no way she was going to buy any shoes, one year of service – an incredible price.

"Yes, prices are getting higher all the time, but . . . "

"When you're dead, you're dead," said Ayesha, and she laughed brightly. What did the price matter?

"Same old, same old," agreed Zach. "What's your name? I've seen you at school, but I'm sorry, I can't recall your name." He smiled his devastating smile. Ayesha didn't mind. She hadn't expected him to know her name, just the fact that he was talking to her was amazing. She had never been so close to Zach before. She was drowning in his attention.

"Excuse me, Sir or Madam." An automaton came up to them. Somehow it had escaped yesterday's transformations. It was still in the body of yesterday's conceit. It wore the body of Victorian butler and its painted face wore a solemn expression.

But Zach was not impressed by its manufactured dignity. "Just look at that old thing, what a wreck."

"What can you do?" said Ayesha. She slowly shook her head when the butler offered her Feeler discount coupons.

"I wonder what it feels like rattling around in there. Still, it's better than being transferred to a colony world, I imagine."

"I imagine so."

"Shall we get out of here, Ayesha? Get some drinks?"

"Okay."

And Zach took Ayesha by the arm, and she was right, his touch was hot.

◊

When she woke her mind hammered into her consciousness

What?

Zach was sitting at a table with his back to her. Ayesha could see that he was connected to the supermarket. He was shopping.

What was?

The clouding pain was dissipating with the fractured images of the night before coming, relentlessly, into view—too many drinks, too much uncontrolled laugher, too much spending on her mother's card.

What was happening?

"What are you doing?" Ayesha spoke quietly. Her voice was furled and distorted by the night's excess.

"I thought you'd have a virgin's card, my dear. But, no. You've been a very bad girl taking your mother's card."

POLLUTO.

Ayesha walked unsteadily towards Zach. There were too many things in the room; piles of clothing were everywhere; toys, books, and boxes of unopened treasures littered the floor. On the screen she could see her mother's name. Zach was using her mother's card. The computer showed a wild spiral of spinning numbers, racking up debt on her mother's card. A debt of service that would need to be repaid by the copy of her mother's personality, transferred into an automaton's body. One month for a new shirt, two months for a watch, one year for a pair of shoes, all debt that would need to be repaid—after her mother's death.

"No. Stop it." She pushed him away from the screen, and typed in the commands to stop the transactions.

The wild spiral of debt ceased.

"What have you done?"

"Used your card, or should I say, your mother's card, to furnish me, for a few more months. Looking like this doesn't come cheap, you know." He stood up and began to gather shirts, shoes, and jewellery into a leather holdall. "The rest will be delivered later."

"But you've spent too much. I never said . . . "

"But you did say, Ayesha. You said I could buy anything. You said you wanted to make me happy, and I'm very happy." The bright screen light illuminated Zach and cast unkind shadows upon his handsome face. "But unlike you, my dear Ayesha, I believe that the things in the supermarket have to be paid for. And I'd prefer not to do it myself."

He stood up and smoothed down his jacket. It showed images from the Viper Colony. The automatons toiled under the strange sun, powered by the brains of dead customers. How much debt had they racked up in their life-time? When would they be released from their manufactured after-life?

"I like you, Ayesha. You've got a certain style. Maybe we can be friends, when you've grown up a little. That's why I'm giving you back the card." He flicked her mother's life card at her.

How many years would her mother have to endure encased in a metal shell, working to service the lives of the living, long after her death?

"What can I tell my mother?"

"Tell her, oh, I don't know . . . Tell her 'when you're dead, you're dead.' She'll appreciate that, I'm sure."

"I'll report you."

"Will you? Taking someone's card carries high penalties. You'll incriminate yourself. Anyway, 'No refunds. No excuses,' remember? They don't care at the supermarket. Believe me; I've done this before, but never with a mother's card. You really are a bad girl, Ayesha." He smiled at her. "I like that."

And he left her with the objects of the night's debauchery of acquisition. Ayesha reached out for her red fur coat. She buried her face in its warm fur, hiding from the inanimate accusation of the objects which surrounded her.

THE END

LEVIATHAN'S TEETH

KELLY BARNHILL

It is not without ironical acquiescence, dear Father, that I compose this letter. When last we spoke, as you doubtless remember, I told you that I would never see you more 'til we meet in our shared torment in Hell—a dreadful thing to say to any man, and more so to a man of Letters, and of the Cloth. For that, I will not apologize. No, Father, I write because, as I now heave my last labored and bloody breaths, I have no more illusions of this broad, beautiful and wicked World. There is no Truth save this: it is Hell where I now go, and Hell where I will once again lay eyes on your dear, detestable face. My only surprise in this matter is that it is *I* that shall wait for *you*, and not the other way around.

Since you are, primarily, an honest man, it is to your good will and sense of duty that I now entrust my story. It pains me greatly that the report which shall reach the eyes of my dear Mother will be no more than a slanderous yarn detailing my supposed predilection to drink, to carouse, and to seek succor, not in the arms of a chaste and holy wife, but rather, engaging in unspeakable perversions in the darker corners of saloons, and in certain houses of ill-repute who deal with men such as I. These things are true, and I would no sooner deny them than I would deny my own hands or my own, delicious mouth. I am, in the end, a creature of pleasure— hedonistic, self-centered and blessedly full of sin. What I will deny is this: The death of my poor Captain was due not to negligence nor drunkenness—by me nor by any living man. And here I must stress *living*. The events that transpired were due to causes most unnatural—a spectoral stranglehold that even our Captain, both Christian and god-fearing, was powerless to overcome or escape.

◊

I have been, for the last fifteen years, forging a living in the meager towns that rim these vast, freshwater seas—the beating heart of our growing Nation. I have been hired on schooners, sloops and barges for my height, my shoulder's girth, and my skills as a seaman. I do not care for the mariner's life, and often seek to avoid it when possible, using my wages to purchase pleasures in the windy byways of Sault St. Marie, or the skeletal mansions of Duluth, or in that city of my soul, glittering Chicago. Not long ago, my purse ran, again, quite dry, and I was forced to face the howling gales and miserable food once again.

I signed as a bowswain on that accursed ship, the *Erie Board of Trade*. Dear God! How a shudder runs across my skin as I write that name! Though in truth, Father, that devil ship was a thing of beauty: a three-masted sloop, freshly tarred, its sails as crisp and unyielding as virgins. I have no doubt that, upon seeing her, your old seafaring legs would begin to quake and you would long, as I did, for the bracing air on the water. I, who cared nothing for the watery life, found myself yearning for the lusty sway underfoot, the rhythmic pulse of strong men at work. I saw her as she approached the port in Chicago. The great Lake was dark as iron with angry swells capped in foam, but that sloop glided into port as though floating on gossamer. Its movements were easy and delicate as it swiveled its rump neatly into its berth. Never have I seen such a seductress! Perhaps, I should have found it odd that nearly her entire crew stomped away without so much as a backward glance, unwilling to sign on for another haul. It was with a pounding heart that I followed the Captain's call for able-bodied men, and signed articles with a sigh. The pay was better than could be hoped, and our articles detailed the quality and quantity of victuals for each man aboard.

The Captain ordered all new seamen on deck just before our journey began. He was, like me, the son of a Methodist minister and retained the dull sobriety of Methodist dress. No silver glinted in the black sweep of his greatcoat. No buckles gleamed on his boots. His hands were white as lilies and twice as soft, except for his fingertips, which had been scrubbed to rosy nubs of raw flesh. These he often displayed as a fine example for the cleanliness expected from his ship's men.

"I am," said he, "a hard man, though fair. Neither idleness nor drunkenness find homes under my watch. We Christian men know that when we stand before our Lord we deserve no mercy, and must instead bear the natural consequences of our short, miserable lives. Men of wickedness face a fate of their own making. Likewise, on this ship, my men can expect no mercy from me. For hard work and clean living, there will be just compensation, full bellies and a warm roof. For those who display insolence, shiftlessness and dereliction, there is first the whip and then the stocks. Am I heard, gentlemen?"

No one said a word, for, to a man, we were skilled seamen who knew when to speak to a captain and when to hold our tongue. However, next to me was a faint gulp, as though the man forced himself to swallow his own mutinous laughter. I slid my eye leftward to catch a glimpse of the man's face. He was Irish, clearly. Even without seeing his foxy hair, which bore witness to his faith, sullied by Heathenism—or worse, *Papism*—I would have known his origins by his smell. The Irish, in my experience, smell universally of earth and loam, as though they were covered in moss. A dark green scent as entropic and given to chaos as the dark forests that our young Nation now seeks to conquer. Whether this is from diet or hygiene or an endemic characteristic in the skin of the Gallic Races, I am powerless to ascertain, but the effect is off-putting to the point of maddening. Men, in my belief, should smell like men and not like unplanted gardens. I remembered, Father, the dark skepticism with which you regarded the Irish—their idolatry, hedonism and lack of morals and public decency. Though all of those qualities are those to which I have joyfully subscribed during my beloved and wasted life, I have retained your dark warnings and aversions to that odd race. The Irishman, I knew—I *knew!*—nearly guffawed at the Captain. I shuddered. To have insubordination this early could be nothing but a bad omen, and I resolved to clarify my luck with salt as soon as the opportunity arose.

The Captain was true to his word and did not tolerate idleness or even thoughts of idleness. We scrubbed and heaved, hauled and knotted, and even mended like women. We slept in shifts of two hours for every ten of work and faced the lash for insubordinate commentary. Were it not for the sizable purse promised at the delivery of our load, we likely would have turned mutineer instead of quietly grumbling sailor.

The closest thing to mutiny was the Irishman, though, since he was the sole member aboard of his strange race, his views were easily marginalized and ignored. Still, in moments when the Captain's eyes were averted or otherwise engaged, the Irishman managed to slip within earshot, preceded always by the pungent smell of earth and growing green.

"It isn't the work that chafes, nor the hours," he said to me as I leaned down to coil the lines and pretended that I did not hear. Undeterred, he crouched to his haunches and leaned into whisper, his mouth near my ear, the mown grass scent of his breath running down my skin. I shook, stood and walked with purpose towards the lower decks, as it was nearly my shift to man the bilge-water pumps. He cornered me between the bulwarks and the stacks of dinghies. "We are men of strength and action," he said as I stared at the ground. "To be treated like dogs is beneath us. And worse, it is beneath the dignity of this gorgeous vessel upon which we are all privileged to work, sweat and groan." I felt the pulse of the waves at my feet and nearly lost my balance. "The captain doesn't deserve a ship as beautiful as

this. Beauty goes to beauty. That is the pattern of things." And God help me, Father, but he was beautiful. In my life I have lived only for pleasure, and fortunately for me, pleasure is easily purchased. Beauty in eyes, lips and heaving chests—not to mention the dark secrets that lurk in the whispering skirts of women and the damp trousers of willing young men—all of these have prices to be negotiated and agreed upon. If I had ever purchased the services of an Irish lass or lad, it was because they had hidden the telltale features of their race for the sake of business. But this young man had wish to hide nothing. His strange lilt lingered gently on his pink tongue. Pink tongue, pink lips, eyes like clover, skin like milk. I shivered.

"A good ship deserves men who honor her. The man who sheds his blood for her welfare will belong to her forever, and she to him. The Captain," he said this as though the word, and not just the man, was foul, "would not have the courage to do such a thing." I wrested myself away from his gaze and resolved to avoid him when possible. I threw myself into my work, hauling, pumping, grinding and grunting until sweat slicked my face and poured onto the ground.

◊

We carried a tonnage of grain and salted pork from Chicago to Cleveland, where we would swap our wares for coal to bring to the iron mines of Duluth. From there, we would bring iron—the skeleton of our Nation's Destiny—to the barons of New York. Our Captain, clearly cognizant of his lack of crew retention, insisted on articles that would not relinquish our wages until we had berthed on the Hudson, unloaded the sloop, scrubbed her down and, like Jezebel, painted a layer of beauty on her tarnished face.

Between Chicago and Cleveland, the Captain's animosity towards the Irishman became manifest. How often had the Captain, upon seeing the deck recently scrubbed by those powerful buck-Celtic arms, proceeded to knock over the slop bucket and demand that the lot be scoured, its putrid stink removed from the discerning noses of the rest of the crew. Before our first stop, the Irishman thrice faced the lash. First for suspected drunkenness (it was quite true, though how and where he smuggled his wares was a mystery that burned for us all. He was quick to produce a bottle, seemingly from nowhere, for a man who needed it, and just as quickly, retract it into thin air. Truly, they are a miraculous race!); secondly for thieving from the Captains special store of sausages (this was also true, for he shared his booty with me at a time when my arms quaked with hunger and exhaustion); the third time, he was whipped for un-Christian behavior. For this, I have no idea what evidence the Captain had, or exactly which element of un-Christianity the Irishman exhibited. What I do know is this: The Captain ordered the Irishman to his knees. The Irishman was young, no more than a boy, really, and as the Captain stood behind him, a boot on either side of his narrow body. The Irishman looked so lithe and fine against the hulking bulk of the Captain's great coat, that, if I hadn't known better, I might have mistook him for the airy elves of old tales, a creature spun of web, wing and starlight.

"Do you," the Captain shouted to the back of the Irishman's narrow, ginger head, "repent? Will you receive your just lashes with a pure heart and thus delight your maker as you never have?" The Captain's face took on an unpleasant purple color and he panted and gasped as though ill. His chins quivered above his high collar and his mouth was quite dry.

The Irishman did not speak. Instead, he tilted his chin to the sky and regarded it with pleased fascination. He breathed deeply and began to whistle a tune the likes of which I have never heard. It followed no musical pattern that I have known from the church's hymnal, or the bawdy ditties of the public houses. It soared high and light as smoke. It tinkled like water over rocks and warbled easy as birdsong. Even as the lashes came down on his narrow shoulders, the music did not stop. The young man never flinched, nor blinked, nor wept. His shirt ripped, his skin swelled, burst and bled, and yet he didn't seem to notice. In that moment, there was only the sky, and the song, and a shadowed smile playing upon the young man's lips.

◊

I have heard that men and women of that dark island have made deals with the residents of the various sections of Hell for special powers that no man (nor woman, for that matter) should ever possess. Immunity to pain, for example. Charms for fish. Unbreakable love knots to snare unsuspecting suitors. I've heard that their babes are suckled by the Atlantic's mewling seals. I've heard that their old simply curl up on their green hillsides and allow their bodies to become stones heavy with living moss. These things, Father, are doubtless true. I, myself, discovered his devilish snare-knots in my bunk and pockets only just before I first tasted that sea-salted skin.

Despite his strange persuasion, despite my aversion to his rich, dark smell, I was powerless against the insistence of that pale, fluttering mouth.

◊

In Cleveland, the Irishman disappeared as we repaired cracks and rubbed fat on the inner walls of the sloop. I, along with the rest of the crew, assumed that he had foregone the passage wages and had opted to seek his luck with another captain. As we hauled coal into the belly of the ship, I thought I heard the faint whistling of the Irishman's strange song, but upon inspection, the song vanished, leaving only an ache in my chest. However, as we slid into the green waters of Lake Erie, we found him, asleep in his bunk, his young face bright with dreaming. The Captain confined him to stocks until we reached the twin sentinels of Cockburn and Drummond Islands where the tug awaited to maneuver us through that devilish channel into Superior.

◊

Doubtless you have heard the stories of the unfortunate ships lost in those terrible depths. They say that the rocks jut out of the waves like the teeth of the Leviathan. This, I regret to say, is more than true. It is also said that the waves of Lake Superior moan with the voices of the waterlogged dead. This is also true. I have heard those moans issuing piteously from the blue lips of lost men. Over these last fifteen years, those moans have haunted my dreams and have rung maddeningly in my ears in moments of idleness. And now, as my red blood seeps around the edges of my bandages, as it spills onto the sheets, as it drips from my mouth, I hear the moans again. Later, when I breathe my last and my body is (uselessly) prayed upon and heaved into the water, my own cold lips will moan upon the dark waves, my own sighs will come crashing against the rocks.

◊

Superior's gales tossed the *Erie Board of Trade* until her virginal sheets grew stained and ragged, and her hull groaned with each crashing wave. We were without safe harbor and had to feel our way blindly through the wind and spray. The Captain stood next to the helmsman, his face pinched blindly into the gale. Our helmsman, may he rest peacefully in his watery grave, performed admirably. He moved by instinct, anticipating the patterning of rocky spines that masqueraded as swells.. The wind roared and gusted and a swell bigger than a whale reared up and crashed onto the deck. The sail cupped water before straining at its pulleys. The halyard snapped sending the mainsail spilling across the deck.

We had assumed that the Captain, rational being that he is, would set two men to furl the downed sail and use the remaining two to guide us to—if not safe harbor, at least a modicum of security against the pressures of the storm. Instead, the captain called for a new halyard to be brought and threaded into the gaff rig. He pointed at the Irishman.

"You," he called over the wind, "Climb." He signaled with his chin to the top of the main mast, where a crow's nest swayed sickeningly against the wind and strengthening waves.

The Irishman didn't move. "I don't think, sir, that you'd like the results of it if I did."

I do not know if this is true, Father, or if it simply my memory playing tricks upon my dying senses. Perhaps it is both. But I swear, as the Irishman stood in the gale, though the thunder and waves crashed about us and though the freezing rain fell in curtains around our poor ship, the Irishman was unmoved. His hair did not blow, nor did his face stream with water, nor sweat, nor fear. In that moment, a colossal wave rocked the sloop sharply to the side. The Captain staggered against the loll of the deck, flailed his arms like a landsman and grabbed hold of the rigging to right himself. Even I, seasoned sailor that I am, nearly toppled over. The Irishman did not move, but simply breathed quietly in the sweet spray of the wretched lake. This, alas, only infuriated the Captain further. He reached into the darkness of his great coat and pulled out his revolver and pointed.

It is strange, Father, how in moments such as these, when the heart pounds and the mind turns time into ice, that the things to which we had earlier been blind suddenly reveal themselves. These things are pinned to my memory now, and each prick bleeds and bleeds. I noticed, for example, that a spangle of freckles floated in the milk white skin of the Irishman's cheeks and nose. I noticed that his right front tooth bore a chip, one that he likely had since childhood. I noticed that his boots had been mended with leather thongs, and that the skin of his neck and forearms had been marked with the tattoos of the cannibals of the Southern Pacific. His foxy curls curved around his green eyes, and, for just a moment, they darted towards me and winked.

"If any man's blood must be shed for the safety of this ship," the Irishman said, "it should be yours, my Captain. If I climb that mast, I will be dead upon my return, and the soul of the ship and all the men aboard will bind to me forever. You can choose this fate, sir, or let it pass." In response, the Captain pressed the barrel of the revolver to the delicate temple of the Irish boy.

Father, if I live to be a thousand, and again a thousand times a thousand, I would never be able to explain my actions to follow. Was it the knotted snare that the Irishman secreted into my pocket that caused me to behave in a manner so rash as to be suicidal. Certainly, I have never been given to courage before, nor have I since. I have only ever acted in my own self-interest, and doing so has given me a comfortable living and the occasional pleasure. This boy for whom I harbored such suspicion and such fascination was nothing to me, and yet, as he calmly faced the barrel of the gun, I could not bear to live in a world in which he was so violently removed. I felt my bowels turn to water and my voice emit from my throat in incomprehensible and guttural cries. I lunged forward, knocked the boy out of the way and faced the gun myself. The Captain, startled, jerked his firing arm in surprise. The gun went off, though slant, burning an angry slice at the edge of my shoulder. I fell back, knocking my head against the base of the mast and knew only darkness for some time.

I awoke from that swoon in my bunk, wounds dressed but bandages soaked through and reeking My lips cracked when I attempted to open my mouth, and my tongue rattled painfully in my mouth like an animated measure of wood. I staggered out of the hold and onto the deck. The rain had stopped, and the winds reduced by half, but the damage from the storm incited a mania of activity across the deck. The captain stood at the helm, barking orders to the men. I did not see the Irishman.

"Awake are we?" the captain shouted. "At last. You'll make up for it with a double shift. We've no time for shiftless layabouts. You'll use that arm." He indicated my bloodied shoulder with a nod.

"Where's the boy," I said, my voice barely a croak.

"Sailor's burial," the Captain said. "Damn fool slipped on the way down and left me short a man. I should have known better than to hire him. Still, it's one less Irishman, and for that the world can rejoice."

I looked out into the gray water, sick with grief. I thought of those pink lips, now blue, blowing those strange tunes into icy bubbles, his fragile bones gentling the rocks. Though in earlier days, I would have agreed with the Captain, I could not be pleased with the loss of that beautiful young man. Even still, I could still smell his green scent, clinging sides of the boat.

An hour later, the winds ceased and the ship drifted. The sky, gray as ashes, did not stir and the water stretched around us, silvery and flat as a mirror. The crew pulled the lines taut, and gazed uncomfortably at the mast where the Irishman climbed and fell.

"It's his doing," they muttered. Every now and again, a man gasped and jumped, claiming a shadow leapt at the corner of their vision.

The Captain set us to swabbing. "Never," said he, "have I seen such a putrid crew," he bellowed. "Never have I seen the filth of the soul manifest itself in filth of the body and filth of the ship. All around us, your sin breeds mold."

At first, I did not think him wrong. After all, I, too, had noticed a poison green fur spreading along the gunnels of the sloop and curling up the mast. It grew across the deck and coated the lines. The men scrubbed and scraped, but the green expanded. It grew thick and cool, pillowing in corners and sprouting clover in the light. I crept closer to the green and ran my fingers across its velvet surface. It was moss. I reached my fingers in and pulled out a handful. It smelled of milky skin and spangled freckles and a single tooth chipped in childhood. What's more, in my hand was more than moss. My fingers pulled a handful of the boat, as well. I leaned in closer inhaled the sweet scent of rotting wood. At the corner of my eye, a shadow grinned.

The sky dimmed and eased without announcement into evening. The Captain ordered measures of salt poured out onto the moss and set men to work with shovels and knives. A man named Alvin Clement had lain down on a pocket of moss. He slept instantly and heavily, and did not wake as the moss crept over his feet, blanketing his legs, hips and chest. His breaths were slow and easy and the moss grew heavy and wet across his neck and face. Were it not for a single nostril unblocked, he would have suffocated.

"Up, man," the Captain shouted, tearing the moss away from the sleeping man's body. Clement gazed up at the Captain, blinking slowly as though he were still dreaming. The Captain rained down blows upon the poor fellow, and whether the effort was to beat the moss away or to simply beat poor Clement to death, I could not say.

"Sinful muck," the Captain shouted as the daylight emptied out of the sky. "Entropy and decay. You will kneel down and beg for forgiveness. You have no place on this ship. It doesn't *belong* to you!" As he shouted he swung his head from side to side, shaking his fist at the air.

Brooks and Guthrie lit lamps, but it only fueled the Captain's rage. The moss obliterated the sails. It covered the deck where it gave way to lengthening grasses, pale yellow flowers, and the sharp scent of peat. I stepped forward to cut another shovel-full of greenery and thickening loam, when an unmistakable crack sounded below me. I peered through the darkness to the Captain, who furiously scoured the helm, and while the moss fell away from it in great hunks, a snaking of ivy twined each spindle to his arm, coiled around his neck like a lover, binding him fast. Ivy grew around Brooks and Guthrie as well while Clement fell back asleep.

The moss grew thick on my boots and the first strands of ivy crept over the soles and into the laces. Quickly, I removed my boots, ran to the dinghy and dropped into the water, rowing as though the devil itself was following. As I rowed, the moon began to rise behind the faintly glowing clouds. The mast, it seemed, sprouted flowers at the top before bending limply to the ground. The sails dissipated in a shower of petals, or pollen or broken leaves. The rotting wood groaned and cracked, the water bubbled and swallowed and smoothed. The clouds above shattered, leaving behind sharp stars, a slash of moon, and the merciless sheen of the moonlight on the dark and utterly empty water. The ship, Father, was gone.

◊

A fishing vessel discovered my craft and my own, barely conscious self. The infection from my shoulder attacked my blood, making it boil and froth. They thought that the shipwreck—for certainly, what other explanation could there be?—had made me mad. I was naked and shivering, and apparently clawing at my body and splashing it with cold water. The fishermen wrapped me in woolen blankets and fed me upon broth and boiled potatoes. We landed in Bayfield, and I gave them the address of the proprietress of a certain House at which I have been a customer over the years. The proprietress, God bless her sinful soul, gave me bed and care while I ailed, and a sampling of her wares when I began to mend. For this she did not charge me, and though neither of us mentioned it, I have a suspicion that the several purses lifted from me by the nimble fingers of the boys and girls of her employ had finally been made honest. Though barely.

◊

I told no one the specifics of the demise of the *Erie Board of Trade*. It is doubtful that I would have been believed. At any rate, my status as a wreck survivor hampered my ability to secure a position on another vessel—one that might, hopefully, return my wanderings to Chicago. I bore the stain of the ill luck and most captains preferred to keep me on land, rather than endangering their payloads and crew with my lack of good fortune. Surely, if I let the entire story be known, I would likely have found myself strapped to a rail as strong men hastily escorted me from town. Still, rumors spread of a ghost ship spotted not far from where the fishermen netted me out of the water. Wherever I went, whispers hung in the air like smoke, and eyes averted. The ship, they said, had a red haired ghost who stood on the shoulders of a bent man in a black greatcoat. They said that the red haired man sang to the calming waves. They said that the ship blew off a scent reminiscent of green forests, green moss, a loamy, unplanted garden.

After several weeks, my hostess felt my presence chafe and gave me notice that when she returned from church that Sunday, she would prefer to find me gone, and would likely bring along a man or two with impeccable aim to ensure that if I was not gone, I would be soon. Fortunately, the following day brought better news: A captain berthed a floundering ship in bad need of repair. I made my skills known, and before he had time to hear my story, engaged my services on the spot.

"You aren't afraid of ghost ships, are you lad?" the captain asked seriously.

I trembled. "Not in the least, sir. Personally, I find the presence of a ghost ship to be no more than a mild challenge to the seasoned sailor."

He slapped my bad shoulder and guffawed mightily. I winced and attempted to guffaw as well. "Good lad," he said. "Half my crew spooked not two hours out of Duluth. The last thing I need is another Nancy."

"No fear, captain," said I. "I'm your man."

◊

We had not been but an hour from port when the Irishman first appeared. I saw him standing on the water, a circle of silvery calm under his feet. I gasped and turned away, hauling like thunder against a wind that evaporated inexorably away. The other sailors noticed the dying wind, looked at me and grumbled quietly to one another through half-closed mouths. They did not see the Irishman, and, when I turned, I couldn't see him either.

We dropped anchor in Whitefish Bay, waiting for our escort through the channel. The sun hung low and red in the darkening sky, and though the ship had been battened and cinched, the men paced the decks searching for something to do. Men scoured clean decks, re-furled sails, rearranged and re-packed stocks and supplies. I, myself, checked and rechecked knots, tightening things that needed none, yet still I paced, unable to eat or drink, unable to sit. We were waiting, ostensibly, for the tug that would see us safely through the channel, and bring me closer to the city of my soul. But we were waiting for something else as well—something that we could not name.

The men leaned against the side of the deck, watching the last shreds of the vanishing sun dissolve into the purple sky. They stared anxiously at the glassy water, muttering to themselves that they had never seen the great Lake so still, that it was unnatural and boded ill. The water stretched away from the boat, first silver, then soft and green as moss. The men drank in the scent, flaring their nostrils and tilting their faces to the sky.

"I know that smell," said one, his face pale and trembling. "I *know* it."

"I smelled it once, when I was a boy," said another. "Sure as hell don't belong here, though." He was right.. Lake Superior smells of iron and smoke. It smells of wet rocks and dry coal—the virile smells of Industry.

What happened next, Father, though I was present and experienced all, remains incomprehensible to me. Even now, as I read the words on this page, smeared as they are by my sinner's tears, sinner's blood, sinner's trembling hands, they read to me as lies—the vanishing fancy of a dying man. I assure you—as I assure myself—that they are not.

The still water darkened and greened. It became deep, rich and fragrant. It was as though the rocky, pitiless bottom of the great lake sighed and moaned with life and love and abundance. From the edge of the ship to the edge of the sky, the water became moss, the moss became clover, and the clover swelled with blossoms. I heard the voice of the Irishman coming from the darkening sky. The song drifted like pollen and landed on the vast gardens at the edge of the ship. Where the song fell, a ship grew. It uncurled from the clover field, its mast unfurled and stretched like stalks, and its sails swelled supple as young leaves. At the top of the main mast, in the very spot where once sat a crows' nest where the Irishman climbed, fell and died, where he, at last, shed his blood for that beautiful ship, there was a swelling bud, an opening flower, and in the center, a bright young man. He sang, and oh! how the tune slicked against my hands, my skin, my delicious mouth. And oh! how I fell to my knees, thanking a God that I barely remembered and barely knew for allowing me the grace to hear such a song. And oh! how my lips trembled and my and my body hungered for a food that came not from earth nor air but from the angel flesh of a heaven that I would never see.

The crew, I later learned, was blind to this vision. They did not see the blossoms or the clover or the flowering mast with a beautiful boy serenading the world. What they did see was this: The shadow of a ship slipping ever nearer, and a haunted old man, on his knees, his arms stretched towards the ghost of a ship, beckoning it nearer. The ship's Mate, in terror and rage, unsheathed his stiletto and plunged it into my solar plexus. I bled; I flowed; I was a river of grass and song and life. I closed my eyes and saw the blush on the Irishman's lips leaning in, fluttering against my forehead. When I opened my eyes, he was gone. So was the ship, the clover, the moss and the song. There was only the jag of stars on a cold swept sky, the crush of water against the rocks and a sea of blood lapping against the deck.

◊

Even now, Father, the nib wobbles in my right hand. My fingers, my feet, my long strong legs lose strength, then sense, then pain. I am, now, more meat than man, and soon, when at last my body sinks into the hidden caverns of the Lake, I will be more muck than meat. Perhaps it was meant to be so.

As I take in these, my last halting breaths, I remember you as the man I knew as a child, the sharp click of boots, the insurmountable great coat, like a black mountain against the sky. I feared your wrath, your fury and your potential for pain, just as I longed for the tender chokehold of my mother's love— the suffocating allure of her bounteous breasts, the net of skirts that pulled me ever near. You have made me the man that I am, and I am grateful for it. Where you sought the merciless severity of a pitiless Faith, I sought out gluttony and drunkenness and unspeakable pleasure and damnable joy. In this way, the world balances itself. In this way, the cesspool flowers and the deadly waters run heavy with fish, blossoms and manly industry. In this way do old men curl to mossy rocks and their children plant gardens over their greening breasts. In this way does my blood flow out of my heart, does it drip like oil into the water, does it become lilies and clover and a living ship, unfurling from the waves, flowering towards the deep, soot-smudged sky.

THE END

78

IN THE DUTIFUL REPUBLIC

TERENCE KUCH

In the dutiful republic we practice our smiles on our uncomplaining mirrors, hold our hands tight over our minds, say only the wrong right things. We concentrate, now, on being public beings, view that which infests us. Which simulation are we, today? Know not how to think,

(contrasting views of responsible spokespersons

{who are however subject to the same illusions as those whose views do not contrast}

are welcome)

but what. I pelvis to the Leader's television'd motions, pretend his tongue is moist and tight inside my ear. In the light we are dutiful; but at night we gather quietly in the home of one or another, cover windows with dark cloth, power-up the peering-machine, watch the Leader address his people. We rub in rhythm against the cold tube. We Tivo it over and over until we can time our brutal movements to the cadence of anointed speech with exquisite and exhausting precision.

There is no pounding at the door tonight because doors are now forbidden.

The mirrors—the mirrors have stopped reflecting us.

THE END

HEART IS WHERE THE HOME IS

MARK HOWARD JONES

In his old, tilting clockwork house at the edge of the town, Framehr lived with his daughter and four cats.

His daughter was so graceful, yet so fickle, and his cats so attentive, with such kindly faces, that he often thought he had four daughters and one cat.

But it was just an old man's imagination getting very much the better of him.

When Framehr's house was new it made hardly any sound, just the murmur of swift-running water over pebbles. Now it was old and badly in need of repair, it made all the fuss and tumult of water streaming into a bowl after a long journey.

The man who had built Framehr's house—a Belgian engineer and architect of worldwide renown—had proclaimed it a marvel and went on to state that everyone would one day live in such well-oiled, self-winding machines.

Sadly, the man was now long dead and no-one knew enough about the house to restore it to full working order.

Many monographs and books about the architect spoke of the wonderful house in an historical context, lamenting that we hadn't followed the path laid out by the Belgian visionary. These same publications always failed to mention the current poor state of the house or its present owner's urgent need of a man talented enough to restore it to its original condition.

Even if Framehr could find an individual with such talents, he would be unable to pay for the repairs that were needed.

Not even Framehr's daughter (or did he have four? . . . ah, well) knew exactly how old her father was, but she did know he'd lived a long and profligate life.

She knew he had, in turn, been a thief, a television performer, a gambler, a doctor and a chef (he had, in fact, cooked greasy meals for greasy dock workers in a grey refinery port for just four months, but Framehr felt the title "chef" conferred upon him an otherwise unobtainable air of creativity).

She also knew he had made, or swindled people out of, a great deal of money but it had all been spent on buying and attempting to maintain the marvellous house.

Anyone who knew about money and what to do with it would have airily dismissed the house as a "bad investment". But Framehr felt it was the one time in his life that he had ever used money wisely, apart from the smaller sum spent wooing his late wife, Julia.

A faded colour photograph showing three people wearing clothes some decades out of fashion hung in the house, forming the fourth side of a square completed by three clocks.

The three people—Framehr, Julia and the brilliant Belgian—are standing in front of the miraculous house, which is purring softly away in the background, biding its time.

The architect would have disapproved of what Framehr and Julia had done to "his" house, stuffing its perfectly *proportioned insides with dusty brown and green furnishings, cluttering its spaces and breaking up its lines. The built-in furniture ought to be enough for even the most demanding tenant, he would have declared, if asked.*

But he never re-visited the house and Julia considered it most demanding of its tenants.

She strove to make it comfortable with Framehr's help. Then their daughter came along and they were all very happy there . . . until Julia died.

◊

Paterson saw the house from some way off, standing up against the skyline. He sailed past the shingle spit that started almost at the door of the house and tied up at a dilapidated jetty some few hundred yards inland.

After he'd stoked down the boiler and the boat was secure, he hefted his heavy leather bag up onto the jetty and climbed out.

He stood looking towards the house for a few moments before lifting his bag up onto his shoulder and setting off towards it. The sprawl of the town ended just a few fields shy of the house. Even from this distance the structure was impressive; four storeys of elegance and engineering perfection, with just a hint of something out of kilter with the three upper floors. If his information was right, as he knew it was, things weren't as perfect as they seemed at first. And that was what he was counting on.

As he drew nearer to the house along the grassed-over path that ran along the shore, he could hear the structure groaning and wheezing to itself. It clearly wasn't happy.

Finding the door of the house open, Paterson went in.

He crossed the living room, patting one of the metallic servants on the head as he passed. The servant made no response, staying where it was, clicking softly and feebly waving its arm at chest level. Once there had been many servants softly humming through the house on thin metal rails which were barely visible, cleaning every room at all hours. Now only a few were in evidence, stopped in their tracks. The others were trapped inside the walls, oblivious to their entombment.

"Oooh," said the young woman as she rounded a corner and nearly bumped into Paterson. Her gaze quickly took in his expensive-looking but crumpled grey clothes and tired manner. "Who are you?"

If Paterson had been wearing a hat he would have taken it off. He smiled at her dark hair, pale cheeks and pretty green eyes. "I'm Paterson. The door was open so I just came in. And what is your name?"

"Eve," she said uncertainly, ". . .and the door's always open. We can't close it."

Paterson nodded slightly. "In that case, I've come to see your father. I think I can help him . . . or perhaps both of you." A small black and white cat rubbed itself against Paterson's legs.

Eve smiled, coolly. "Hmmm. Let's go and find him, then." Paterson spent the time they were searching admiring Eve. Her precise, swift walk and the curve of her back where it met her buttocks made him imagine how she must move during lovemaking. It was certainly a distraction, but a pleasant one.

They finally found the old man in his study. He was seated behind his desk, shuffling through papers and absent-mindedly stroking a cat in his lap. Now and then, he ran his fingers through the wispy white hair that clung to the sides of his head.

"Father. This gentleman has come to see you."

Framehr lifted his gaze and peered at Paterson. "Hmmm. Hello. What is it you want? I'm not *buying* anything, if that's what it is."

Paterson stepped around Eve and extended his hand; it was ignored. "I'm not selling anything, sir. My name is Paterson and I understand from your daughter that you need some help with the house. I'd be very interested in helping you." He was aware of appearing over-eager.

The old man looked at him oddly. "You *want* to help with the problems we've been having with this house?"

Paterson nodded. "I believe I can help, yes. I'm an engineer."

Picking the cat up from his lap and placing it on the floor, Framehr took a step towards the younger man. He nodded. "Well, why don't you stay for dinner? We can talk about it then."

◊

Over dinner, after essaying the basic problems facing the house, it was clear that Framehr wished to discuss "terms".

He leaned forward. "So are you a successful engineer, Mr Paterson?"

Paterson finished chewing another mouthful of the frugal meal. "Well, I'm an engineering student. But I'm in the Honours class and I'm about to graduate. I'm a huge admirer of Van Epps' work, you see."

The old man smiled. "Yes, yes. You said." Framehr looked at his daughter and she gazed back at him, almost as if they were speaking to each other without words.

Framehr sighed and spread his hands in front of him, as if indicating to his visitor that he had nothing to hide. "I have no money to pay for any repairs, Mr Paterson. I spent most of what little wealth I had commissioning Van Epps to design and build this house. Now there is nothing left."

Paterson smiled at him. "I'm not asking to be paid, sir. All I ask is that you let me take some photographs of the repair process in order that I may write a book about it. It would be a prestigious project for me. And the payment from any publisher for such a book would more than meet my costs."

Nodding and smiling, Framehr lifted his glass and tipped it slightly in Paterson's direction. "With pleasure," he murmured and then drained it dry. From across the table, Eve parted her thin red lips and smiled at them both.

◊

The next morning, Framehr showed Paterson what he grandly referred to as his library. The small room had a built-in table and chair with a few bookshelves recessed in the walls.

Paterson spent some hours perusing three yellow-covered volumes written in Van Epps' distinctive handwriting. He then unfolded the mechanical diagrams that described how the house worked. But none of it revealed what Paterson was really interested in and what he had come here to find.

An initial inspection of the house proved unsatisfactory, too. He knew from the books that the main structure of the house was cast iron; he wasn't expecting it to have been applied in such elaborate and imaginative ways, but that couldn't be the whole story.

After he had finished poring over the books and touring the house, he fetched his lamp from his leather bag and descended to the basement. It was a large room with the usual discarded suitcases and household clutter lying around. After moving some boxes, he found the steel access plate to the heart of the house—the machine pit.

Once he'd got the plate off, Paterson put his head through the opening and held his lamp over the open space below. A cursory glance around the machine pit told him that his pretence of fixing the house's mechanisms would have to be just that; the corrosion and wear were considerable. There was a ladder fixed to the wall just inside the opening but he didn't feel like descending into that rust-flaked sinkhole just yet. The most he could hope to do was to replace one or two minor parts and grease some of the more accessible gears. It should be enough to convince the old man that he knew what he was about.

Yet he was puzzled. Parts of the house rotated to follow the sun, while there was a complex system of vents and ducts to regulate the temperature inside.

But there was no evidence in the machine pit of the advanced hydraulics that would be necessary to power these systems. And he doubted if questioning Framehr would bring him any answers. He would have to search harder, pry deeper.

◊

Over the coming days Paterson made sure he appeared before Framehr or Eve from time to time with his shirt sleeves rolled, holding a spanner or some other useful-looking tool, and with an appropriate amount of rust or grease smeared over his face and arms.

This, together with statements like "Well, Van Epps might have been a genius but he counted without the corrosive properties of this salt air", were a necessary sleight of hand. It served to head off any awkward questions about his "progress" in repairing the house.

In his last few interviews Van Epps had referred to his greatest creation being *within* the house. He'd used tantalisingly unclear phrases like "my greatest creation" and "the promise of a new beginning". Yet nothing Paterson had seen so far came anywhere close to the hyperbole of the architect's words.

Some innovations were impressive—like the furniture that rotated into the walls for storage, or the "stored sunlight" lamps used in the bedrooms—but he was certain they weren't what his employers were paying him to find. The cabal of wealthy collectors and eager museum curators had been unable to tell Paterson exactly what he was looking for but, based on Van Epps' comments, he was sure it was sufficiently impressive that he'd know when he found it.

◈

The more he saw of Eve over the following weeks, the more he realised that he didn't wish to rush his task. He found her precise movements alluring, yet she was only ever pleasant but cool towards him. This added to his fascination with her.

She always wore simple dresses that showed off her body without being exactly inviting. He sometimes waited around corners simply in order to watch her walk towards him or away from him, admiring her curves as she passed near him.

Soon his sleeping hours were filled with lustful dreams of Eve. He was sure she was a virgin; locked up here with her father, she never seemed to go further than the garden.

He wanted her and knew he might have to resort to some sort of subterfuge in the first instance.

Paterson thought first of hiding in her room in order to surprise her, but the clockwork locks on the bedroom doors were fiercely difficult to work out and resisted his best efforts to pick them. They could only be opened by the room's occupant, it seemed. But he wasn't going to give up, convinced that once he was within Eve's hideaway she would accept him as her master, if only for one night.

◈

One afternoon Paterson was examining the door to Eve's room, searching for any weakness in the design, when, before he knew anything, she was at his elbow.

"Mr Paterson?"

He felt his heart stick in his throat. "Oh, Eve. Hello." He forced the words out past the obstruction.

She seemed completely unconcerned at his presence outside her bedroom door. "I've been looking for you. I want to show you something. Out in the garden."

Paterson was sure he was blushing. "Oh, right. Yes."

They descended the broad curved staircase side by side and Eve led Paterson through the large doors at the back of the house.

Though he desired her, he hated her mystery; the atmosphere of the arcane she tried so hard to weave around herself. The act of the unattainable virgin, the unstained waif devoted to her arts and to her ageing father, made him sigh audibly as he followed her.

She glanced over her shoulder at him. "What's wrong?"

Raising his eyes to meet hers, Paterson found himself entranced by a dance of unexpected movement and colour. The bright, lovely garden came as a surprise after the harsh and measured interior of the house.

Eve had turned to face him. "Are you alright?"

"Yes, mmm." His eyes struggled to drink in the variety of forms and textures that met them. The garden was vivid with movement in the light breeze, and the colours seemed too intense for the weak spring sunlight.

As he followed Eve towards an oddly-shaped structure partly hidden at the bottom of the garden, Paterson caught a glimpse of something shining among the flowers and plants.

He stepped closer to where the light had caught his eye, reaching forward to part the leaves of a rose bush, cautious to avoid the cruel thorns.

"What are you doing?" Eve had retraced her steps and was standing just behind him.

Paterson started. "I thought . . ."

"Yes, I see. The plants are just weeds—they sowed themselves, you know." It was obvious that Eve thought her explanation full enough and continued on her way to the strange building.

Paterson took the opportunity to peer more closely at what hid in the foliage. There, among the burning colours and lush greenery, stood rows of neatly-aligned steel stalks. Their heads were made of burnished petals studded with bright gems. A metal garden! Of course, thought Paterson. It made sense that Van Epps would extend his architectural theories to the grounds as well as the house.

But he could not think how the metal and the precious stones remained untarnished and bright among the organic lushness that surounded them.

Paterson quickly caught up with Eve. She turned as he touched her on the shoulder.

"Weeds? You said the flowers were weeds?"

She blinked at him but her expression remained unchanged, as if she was dealing with a slow child.

"Yes. There were none when the house was built. The garden looked lovely when it shone in the sun. But now. . . " She looked around at the generous growth sadly. "It's been choked. I thought you knew. You said you could help."

None of the books or architectural monographs Paterson had read had even mentioned the garden. Architects! Now if the volumes had been written by horticulturalists . . . but then again . . .

"I didn't know. I-it's incredible," stumbled Paterson.

Eve smiled slightly at him before turning away to continue her journey.

Once they'd reached the unusual gazebo at the end of the path, they sat each side of a small wooden table covered with a dark cloth and some wind-gathered detritus.

Eve reached inside her dress pocket and removed a set of large cards. She spread the cards on the small table before her, ignoring the leaves that covered part of it.

"What's this?" asked Paterson.

"They're cards."

Paterson sighed with soft impatience. "I can see that. If you want me to play, you'll have to teach me the rules. I'm not big on card games."

Eve gave a short laugh. "It's not a game. Well, a game of sorts, I suppose."

Still puzzled, Paterson directed his best quizzical look in her direction.

Eventually she responded. "They're for cartomancy . . . looking into the future, if you like."

"Witchcraft, now?!" he snorted.

Eve shook her head, looking slightly hurt. "No, no. I'm no witch, just a sensitive, that's all." She smiled at him, then flipped the first card. "The Huntress'."

POLLUTO.

She turned the second. "Ah, 'The Lost Island'," she said with mild concern.

Paterson looked from the cards' hand-painted designs to Eve's intent small face. "Well?"

"It means that you may not get all you hope for. But the later cards could put a different complexion on things. Let's see." She plucked absent-mindedly at the front of her dress as she spoke, inadvertently releasing one of the buttons.

She laid the next two down without comment—"The Tattered Banners" and "The Burdened Priest"—and, even though he didn't believe in anything that the cards said, Paterson became vaguely concerned.

A further two cards—"The Saltimbanque" and "The Morning Star"—joined the pattern laid out before them. "Hmmmm," said Eve. "I think I see."

"And this card," she flourished it before setting it down, "shows your true desire." She set it in its place and frowned. Paterson read the words "The Mare's Delight" at the top of the card and noted the elaborate design of two horses copulating beneath a lunar eclipse.

He smirked at her, but her eyes were intent on the pattern that the cards made on the table. "The Seneschal", "The Crowded Cell", "The Hungry Man", "The Smiling Sisters", "The Burning Tree" and "The Almoner" all came out of the pack and went on to the table.

Eve looked up suddenly and met Paterson's eyes. She began to laugh.

"What? What is it?" he asked. The girl simply kept on laughing. Paterson let this continue for a few more moments but then began to feel as if he were being made a fool of. He leaned forward and angrily brushed the cards from the table. "Damn the cards . . . and damn you!" he hissed.

Eve stopped laughing and looked at the cards scattered on the floor with slight disdain. When she lifted her eyes to Paterson, her gaze was cold.

Feeling suddenly ashamed, Paterson picked the cards up carefully and shuffled them into a neat pack once more.

"I'm sorry," he said. " I just . . ."

She lifted her head, her deep green eyes staring straight into his. "Can I be honest with you, Mr Paterson? Shall

I tell you what the cards revealed to me?" He nodded, eager to repair whatever damage he had done; he feared it was considerable.

"I don't think you've been honest with us. I don't think you want to repair our house and to write a book about it at all. You want something else from us, don't you? I don't think you should deny it. But should I tell my father or not?"

Paterson felt stunned. Was the question genuine, he wondered. He could simply deny his true intentions, but he was intrigued to find out if he had another way out.

"What do you mean?"

◊

Paterson had never met a woman like Eve before. She'd simply stated clearly and simply what she wanted; no games, no coquettishness. She'd told him that she'd seen the way he'd looked at her and that she wanted him to come to her room and take her virginity that afternoon. That way his secret would be safe with her, she'd said.

He'd been taken aback by her offer. He had no way to know if he could trust her, but he wasn't about to turn down her offer either. Besides, he reasoned that she probably wouldn't want her father to find out about their "meeting", so he'd have a hold over her after this.

At four o'clock Paterson stood outside her door. He was about to knock when he noticed it had been left open for him. He entered cautiously. Looking around the room, which was more ornately decorated than the rest of the house, he noticed Eve's bed in a large recess to one side. It was covered in white lace curtains, which hid it from the rest of the room.

When he drew back the lace he found Eve already undressed and in bed. She smiled at him coyly, with the bedclothes pulled up to her chin. Suddenly she threw back the sheets to show herself to him. Paterson's breath caught in his throat. He'd only seen four women's bodies before—and one of those was a saggy old whore his father had hired to "break him in"—but Eve was far more beautiful than any of them. Her body was as pale and promising as he'd imagined it; each curve promised him more than the last.

She seemed neither excited nor dismayed at the prospect of losing her virginity, merely lying there passively. "Now. Please."

Struggling to control his desires and not make a fool of himself, Paterson quickly discarded most of his clothes and lay on the bed next to her. They began to kiss as he ran his hand over her body. She shivered slightly and he thought perhaps she was cold. She moved her legs apart for him and he moved his body between them, freeing his hard penis from his underclothes at the same time.

At the sudden downward pressure of his body, her cunt cracked open in a confusion of cogs and counter-springs.

Paterson gasped in pain as sharp metal cut into his lower belly. He leapt from the bed and grabbed at a pillow, pressing it against the wound to staunch the flow of blood.

Eve looked at him one last time, surprise in her expression as her lips weakly framed the words "I love . . . " There was an awful sound of liquids settling and pressure hissing free and then she lay still, her limbs disjointed and awry. A sharp cracking sound accompanied the opening of her body from groin to breastbone as machinery and tubing forced its way out.

Stunned by what he saw, Paterson felt he should bundle the machine girl up as he would a human corpse. Something at the back of his mind told him this was the right thing to do. He grabbed the sheets either side of Eve and pulled them over her, to the accompaniment of further hissing and the odd soft pop.

He dressed quickly, stuffing a bunched pillow case against his wounded stomach, and scooped the exquisite clockwork girl up in his arms. As he carried her carefully down the stairs, he found tears wetting his cheeks and blurring his vision.

She was the marvellous thing that Van Epps had hinted at. The clue had been there in her name all along; she was the new Eve, the first of her kind. And the last.

◊

Paterson eventually found Framehr in the basement, hunting for a box of old papers.

When he saw Paterson carrying something wrapped in a sheet, he stopped what he was doing and walked over to him. "What . . . ?" He reached forward and uncovered Eve's face.

"She was . . . mechanical," was all Paterson could think to say.

Framehr let out a wail and tried to strike Paterson. "You killed her! You killed her, you bastard! Give her to me, give her to me, give her back!" Paterson extended his arms so that Framehr could lift the figure from him.

Idiotically he repeated: "She was mechanical."

Framehr's eyes blazed at him. "I *know* what she was. She was my daughter. Julia and I couldn't . . . It took Van Epps years . . . years . . . " He sobbed, holding the machine's hair to his face for a moment before laying the body gently on the floor.

"I came looking for her," confessed Paterson. "Even though I didn't know it."

This seemed to make sense to Framehr. He gave a short, bitter laugh. "So you knew. Well, you're not the first to come looking for Van Epps' secret masterpiece! What did they offer you for finding it, eh? What will they give you, now that you've destroyed it?"

Paterson shook his head. He stared at the floor. "You hated it here, didn't you? You were both trapped here."

Framehr's face turned red as he became even angrier. "Yes. But if you'd done what you said you would, you fraud, I could have sold this place and lived out a proper life elsewhere! I shouldn't have trusted you so easily. You haven't done a single thing since you've been here, have you?"

"But what about her? Could she have lived anywhere else?" Paterson asked, nodding vaguely in the direction of Eve's remains.

The old man's face dropped. He half-turned away, as if he'd suddenly remembered an unfinished task, before looking back at Paterson and nodding once.

Framehr staggered back a few paces. He bent and scooped the thing he'd called his daughter from the floor. A look of immeasurable sadness crossed his face as he moved towards the opening to the machine pit.

Despite his age, he hopped quickly onto the ladder, cradling the disintegrating form of Eve in his arms. Paterson heard small metal parts dropping into the pit, clattering on the floor. Framehr looked back at him, an expression of awful loneliness on his face.

"What? What are . . . ?" Then Paterson realised and dashed forward. He stretched his arms through the opening, trying to grab Framehr. But the old man had already jumped, his mechanical daughter clutched to him, plunging down into the darkness and rust and relentless motion of the dark pit. Paterson heard something hit the huge wheels and cogs, then came a strangled scream and the sound of gears straining against something less yielding than flesh and bone.

He tried to peer down into the pit but a cloud of rust and darkness rose to meet him. Shielding his eyes, he turned away as the floor began to shake and rivets complained and then popped. Ripping through the threadbare carpets, the giant metal plates of the floor began to tilt and crumple as the machinery of the house tore itself apart. Paterson ran for the stairs.

Once upstairs, he ran through the lurching structure and almost leapt out of the front door. He threw himself on the sparse grass and hid his face from the cloud of dust and debris rolling out from the grinding, groaning despair of the house.

After ten minutes, the noise subsided and Paterson dared to raise his head. He felt sick as he saw that Van Epps' masterpiece was now a tumbled and tangled heap of metal, rust, sticks of wood and God alone knew what else. He stood and walked over to it. The house seemed to have toppled over backwards, away from where he had lain, revealing the machine pit and another room hidden beneath the structure.

He knelt, fascinated, and peered in. He hadn't discovered this other, hidden room during his examination of the house. It contained two huge tanks and an elaborate pumping system; the hydraulics that Paterson *knew* had to exist. A metallic smell rose from the room and, as he watched, the tanks began to leak a red liquid onto the floor of the secret room. Soon the room was full and it began to spill over the lip onto the grass at Paterson's feet. The body of one of the cats floated in the liquid.

He sniffed suspiciously, then bent to test some of the fluid with his fingers. He recoiled at the smell. It was blood. *Blood?!* Paterson's head reeled. The house was alive but the girl was a machine—was that it? Was this bizarre reversal Van Epps' great secret? And what about the old man—was he just an old man? Or another of Van Epps' "toys"?

Paterson looked quickly at the other subterranean space now opened to the revealing daylight. In the back of his mind, he hoped Framehr had survived and that he'd be able to reveal everything Paterson needed to know.

As soon as he looked down into what had been the machine pit, Paterson knew he wouldn't be getting any answers.

But there, in the midst of of the tangled flesh and torn machinery, an eye of deep green stared out at him from a perfect, pale face. It must have been the way the light from the setting sun caught it, or maybe he'd got a speck of rust in his own eye, because it *couldn't* have winked at him.

THE END

Anarchy in the UK

by Micci Oaten

narchy in the UK is quite an appropriate title for my piece, as I feel this may just be what will happen very soon if the state of our society does not change for the better.

I am boiling inside, as I am sure you are too when watching the news, because I do not feel I have a voice anymore as a British person and I feel like a second class citizen in the eyes of my own government.

Everyday I see people scared to speak out in case someone screams an 'ism' in their face. Oh, how programmed we are by the powers that be to keep us in our place! Our freedom of speech is being smothered by insidious cowards in positions of authority. Our councils point out every difference between people, and they walk on egg shells so much they end up offending everybody. For the record, most people do not care what colour you are or how you dress—this is meant to be 2009 AD not 2009 BC! Our freedom of speech is slowly being taken from us under the guise of protection.

There will always be people who are far behind the times and don't like progress, but they are only expressing their own fears and feel threatened by change. We have come a long way from tribalism, but I am not convinced our councillors have caught up yet, when they continue pointing out differences and rewarding people for being what they class as a minority. I am offended when I need to fill out a form and I am asked my ethnicity and colour. Why should this matter? I am a British citizen. No one is a minority and no one should be treated as such. We should be treated as one with no segregation. If you are British and live within this society and culture, is this too much to ask or am I dreaming?

We are made to believe, by the media, that we cannot fly our own flag and be proud to be British, because this offends? Are we not offended by the civil serpents telling us we should stop being British and hide who we are to please others? I know a lot of people who are proud to be British, so why should we hide it?

Now we are all racists if we are proud to be British, and you are accused of being part of the National Front. How ridiculous! So the Queen is now a racist flying the flag every morning from her palace? The USA proudly flies its flag every morning in its schools and places of work, singing *The Star Spangled Banner*. So do many other countries and so should we!

I am sick and tired of being crushed and trodden upon by our Government. By reactively legislating against free speech, in their recent laws against incitement to hatred and whatnot, they're nannying us into submission. They believe we will tolerate anything they want to throw at us—when will this stop? The apathy in this country is enormous, but I do believe it's slowly turning around as people are no longer distracted from the state of the nation by their own materialism (they now have very little money due to the recession). They are starting to open their eyes and see beyond themselves, to realise what a mess we are in and what truly matters.

It has already started with the recent strikes as we are all desperately trying to keep hold of our jobs—not tolerating companies sacking us. Next, I hope they take to the streets to save our liberty. Or do we have to rely on comedians like Rowan Atkinson to speak up for us instead?

A very close friend of mine often pops round for a drink on a Sunday evening, and we sit with a bottle of wine putting the world to rights. In my circle of friends, we all strongly believe if we have a very hot summer, not only will we all feel the temperature of the weather, we will feel the heat of temperaments. There will be more strikes and possibly riots of frustration, simply the British are getting sick of being disempowered by the people they themselves elected, thanks to our Government being afraid. Or is something more dangerous going on in our Houses of Parliament? Is this how they make the people placid? And what if the reaction against their nannying creates an upsurge for organisations like the BNP? Isn't that something to think about?

I have often ranted about the British going abroad only to expect the country we're visiting to serve us fish and chips. This is disrespectful to any culture. When you go to Spain, you eat paella and absorb the local culture, or why are you there? You should have stayed at home and booked a holiday in Blackpool.

If you go to another country and you love the culture and people, maybe you will consider moving there, which will involve learning their language and respecting their laws.

The Government and councils are causing segregation as they overemphasise difference beyond its merits. Difference shouldn't be fetishised in box-ticking, and it shouldn't be used as an excuse to take from us our rights. Difference should, instead, be recognised as the culturally-enriching quality it is.

What I do not understand is why the Government tolerates freedom of speech from people who live amongst us who hate our very existence, and yet not those who might want to respond? For example, the laws against incitement to religious hatred might hinder those wanting to criticise Islamic extremists, or Christian fundamentalists who exploit arcane inferences in their religious texts to criticise others for their sexual preferences, their personal choices or their lifestyles. Can we not criticise these beliefs in return? Conflict, in this sense, is not necessarily a bad thing.

What I do believe in is equality, not have one rule for one person and for this to be changed to suit someone else. I take people as I find them; if they are kind to me, then I am kind to them. If they abuse me, then we are supposed to have laws that will protect me. But to stop people criticising me altogether?

As you can tell, I am not part of the 'PC brigade' that has allowed us to be walked over. Those people believe in 'doing the right thing', which usually means neutrality. In trying to prevent conflict of any kind, they're denying us the right to challenge and question, which is also denying us the right to grow and change. These are things our country needs if we are to become proud again.

There are no egg shells to break; people are using 'isms' for their own gain. We are being demeaned, disrespected and disempowered. Give us enough credit to let us hold opinions and air them; give us the chance to stand up for what we believe in and criticise that which we do not. Give us back control of our own country!

CLOWNING AROUND

JON PECK

Troupe Tremble had everything an eight-year-old boy would expect: unicycles, tightropes, and facepainted smiles as red and exaggerated as their rubber shoes. They burst onto the stage in a fit of exuberance, plastering the stage and each other with cream pies, seltzer, confetti. Jimmy Wiffle should have been every bit as excited as his little sister, Jenny, who alternately giggled and screamed in his mother's arms; but all Jimmy could focus on was the clown car. The sheer physics of the matter fascinated him. All their other antics could be explained away as specific applications of manual dexterity or deception. But the clown car itself amazed him: no matter how he tried, Jimmy could not conceive how twenty-three men in puffy polka-dot suits, a pair of leotard-clad child gymnasts, and a tiger could all fit into a Volkswagen Beetle.

Mrs. Wiffle had her hands full with Jenny. The little one was only just starting on solid food, and if her mother's hunch was right, would need to be changed within the hour. But Jenny hadn't noticed yet. The clowns kept her rapt, then gleeful, then terrified, then rapt again in a cycle which repeated every few minutes. Mrs. Wiffle was so engrossed in her daughter's reactions that she entirely forgot about her son's existence for a brief while . . . long enough, at least, for Jimmy to wander off into the crowd surrounding the center ring. He shuffled across the dirt floor, ducking under the bridges of limbs which attached man to wife and parent to child, poking his way around and occasionally through the adults' legs, in search of his target.

The clown car was parked on the north side of the ring, next to the tent's back entrance; it was a "New Beetle" or a "New VW Bug", phrases Jimmy recognized from his mom's description of her own car. Jimmy could see her across the ring, and ducked quickly behind the car before her gaze swung is his direction.

At first, he wasn't sure which end was the front; viewed from the side like this, the Bug was nearly identical on both ends, a shiny silver curve topped by dark one-way glass. Only the seam and handle of the driver's-side door and mirror broke the shape's symmetry. Jimmy gripped the handle with both hands and pulled hard. It swung open just far enough for him to slip inside, quickly turning around, and tug the door back into the closed position, or nearly so.

The noises of the crowd diminished immediately. He had done it! Jimmy was alone, looking out at the swarm of humanity, relishing his newfound secrecy in this public space. He could observe the show through the dim windshield, but could not himself be seen. Outside his vehicle, the crowd cheered for their favorite comic antics, but their sounds barely penetrated his world.

Jimmy turned, letting his eyes roam about the interior. Even on the inside, it was a lot like his mom's car: grey fabric seats, smooth black dashboard with bulky protruding circular dials, some with one red needle, some with more. No fuzzy heart hung from the mirror, though, and there was a distinct lack of plastic toys littering the passenger seat. In fact, the car's interior was remarkably barren. Maybe, Jimmy pondered, there would be something more interesting in the back seats. He turned in place, preparing to scramble over the center console—and that is when he noticed the shimmering wall of silver which bisected the automobile, blocking his path to the back seats. It pulsed in place, a vertical ocean of opaque fluid extending to the edges of the vehicle's interior.

How funny-looking, thought Jimmy, launching himself into it.

◇

Pogo kept his ears open while he strolled, listening for the sound of any feet but his own echoing from the sidewalk behind him.

"One missed throw" he muttered. "One simple mistake and they stick me with guard duty for the week. Lucky I don't plant a car bomb on them myself, they are." Blast, he was in a foul mood. He kept moving. A little exercise would clear his mind.

His ears perked up as the characteristic slap of a rubber shoe sounded on the walk, less than a block behind. Pogo didn't break his stride. Keep it cool, he reflected, reaching into his shirt pocket for a banana. Don't change pace; if you bolt, he'll pounce.

The banana was just what he needed. He finished downing the sweet fruit, barely overripe, as a van rounded the corner at full speed. Glancing askance at the mirror of a parked car, he

double-checked his aim and casually tossed the banana peel over his left shoulder. Perfect.

His pursuer didn't have time to react. The peel landed just as his shoe came down, sending his foot skidding out from under him. He lurched sideways into the street an instant before the van reached the same location; there was a screeching of tires followed by a dull thump, and a mop of curly orange hair flew up onto the hood.

Pogo broke into a run as he turned into the next alley, resuming a normal pace only when he could no longer hear any trace of angry commotion over the hum of city streetlamps. Damn, the opposition was getting closer. Another month and they'd have figured out which house to go for; his troupe would have to move all over again.

Pogo cut down one more alley, pulling his garage door opener from his pocket.

◇

Jimmy found himself back in the driver's seat of the Beetle. Confused, he glanced back at the wall of silver. Concentric ripples played across its surface, spreading outward from Jimmy's ankle. He pulled it through, and the wall uttered an audible *burp* as it undulated once more and then quieted.

He clambered out of the Volkswagen, attempting to kick the door shut behind him, and landing on his butt for his troubles. The cold concrete floor leeched heat through is jeans as he gazed up at his surroundings.

Above him, the steel track of an electric garage opener rumbled, pulling the flexible door up into the roof. Jimmy gazed out onto an unfamiliar street.

◊

Concealed in the shadows across from his building, Pogo glanced up and down the street: no sign of any vehicles or people approaching. He triggered the garage remote, jogged to the opposite sidewalk, and was about to slip into under the opening door when he noticed a flicker of movement inside. Wary, he flattened himself against the side of the garage; nobody was due home for at least another day. Had the house been compromised already?

He pulled a #2 steel juggling club out of his pack and twisted the handle, exposing its knife-edge. Holding his right heel in place with the left foot, Pogo slipped his size-14 foot out of his size-16 shoe, then repeated the procedure on the other side. Stocking-footed, he crept around the corner, raising his club to strike.

◊

Pogo and Jimmy sat across the kitchen table from each other. Jimmy pouted, picking grit out of his scratched knees. Pogo held a cotton pad to his ankle, absorbing the blood which still flowed from the child-sized bite wound, and attempted to press an ice pack to his groin with the opposite hand. He couldn't decide which would do more damage: frostbite, or inflammation of the bruised area.

"Where in Frizzle's name did you learn to kick like that?" asked Pogo. "Did you father abuse you or something?"

Jimmy stared back, his pout turning to stony anger.

"Okay, okay. Forget I said anything. Look, I'm sorry I freaked you out." No response. "Fine, don't talk. Meanwhile . . . it's my dinnertime. You hungry? Right. I'm gonna make some mac-n-cheese." He stood delicately and limped over to the kitchen, not yet trusting his damaged ankle. He leaned up against the sink, filling a pot with water. "Can you toss me a box of the stuff? Its all the way over there." Pogo pointed to a pantry on the opposite side of the room.

Reluctantly, the boy rummaged through the shelves as Pogo looked on from afar. "Careful! Don't touch any of those brown bottles. You won't have any tolerance to the stuff yet. The mac-n-cheese is on the bottom shelf, in the blue boxes."

Jimmy finally located them and tossed a box over the table at the clown, followed quickly by another.

So the lad is hungry after all, reflected Pogo, *even if he won't speak to me yet.* "Bowls are in the cupboard to your right. Napkins too."

◊

Jimmy awoke in an unfamiliar room. He didn't remember falling asleep. The creepy-looking clown had made them both dinner; it had been delicious, mixed just barely enough so that a few pockets of cheesy dry powder remained trapped between the noodles, ready to break open when he munched down on them. There had been a funny aftertaste, though, and the next thing he knew . . . he was here, waking up on top of one of a half-dozen bunk beds strewn across the room.

He pushed off the bunk, sheets and blanket still made up and only a little wrinkled from his nap on top of them. In the half-dark, he wandered among the bunks, reading the names engraved on each pair: Buttons, Bobo; Tatters, Topsy; Skippy, Stitches. A dresser in the corner was overflowed with wigs, all in the same garish shade of purple that the club-wielding freak had been wearing in the garage. He tried one on; it itched.

Bored, Jimmy leaned up against the door to his room, pressing an ear against the wood. Hearing nothing, he slowly turned the knob and pushed. Nothing moved. He tried again, leaning his full body weight against it. Still nothing. Finally, he backed up and ran headlong at the door, turning at the last second to slam his shoulder against it.

Ouch. That was dumb, he thought to himself, sliding down the door to lean against it.

◊

Hours after the morning light had begun spilling into his room, Pogo finally woke. He swung his legs off the bunk, testing his ankle. It was still tender, but would take his weight. He'd better baby it for a day or two.

104

Baby. Right, the kid. He was probably starving by now; children had fast metabolisms, didn't they?

Pogo ambled over to the other bunk-room, where the other half of the troupe would be sleeping, except that they were all still out—*without him,* Pogo kept reminding himself. *No matter. When they come back and see that I've acquired a new member, they'll remember how valuable I am.*

He unlocked the door and opened it slowly; Jimmy slumped down onto the floor as he did, still half-asleep. His eyes crept open and, seeing the clown looming over him, he came fully awake. His teeth lunged at Pogo's ankle, but this time, the clown was ready; he merely lifted his foot and stepped aside, letting Jimmy throw himself face-first into the hallway.

Pogo placed a foot against Jimmy's back, pinning him down. "Let's be good today, okay? I won't underestimate you again." Jimmy struggled for a bit. Once he had exhausted himself, the boy nodded, admitting defeat. "Alright then. Come to breakfast."

◊

Pogo spent the morning teaching Jimmy about poisons. It seemed a good place to start, lest the child accidentally open—or even handle—one of the wrong bottles in the cupboard and knock himself off.

"You never know what sort of nasty thing is going to be concealed in a cream pie; knives and explosives aren't uncommon. But most often, they contain some kind of poison . . . often a contact poison, on that can affect you just by touching it."

"The thing about most poisons," he continued, "is that we can build up a tolerance: by taking a tiny bit each day, we make our bodies used to the poison. Then if someone gives us a lot of it, the poison won't kill us. Makes sense?"

Jimmy nodded enthusiastically. Creepy or not, the clown had some interesting things to show him. In his own home, anytime he'd come across a bottle of bleach or drain cleaner with the characteristic skull-and-crossbones warning, his mother had shooed him away from it.

Pogo held up a bottle. "This is very dilute cyanide, meaning that this bottle is mostly water, with only a little bit of the poison called cyanide. Even a few drops of this can kill you; but if I take just a tiny but and put it in a whole

105

glass of water . . . " he did so. "Then I can drink it without any problem. Of course, it does have a few side effects." Pogo pulled at his the skin on his grey-white face. "I'm not wearing any makeup, you see."

He described the contents of each bottle to Jimmy, describing how much each clown would take on a regular basis, and the expected side effects—from disproportional bone growth to permanent pupil dilation—of each. He quizzed the child afterwards. The boy's recall was less than ideal; perhaps it was time to move on to physical violence, for which Jimmy seemed to have a knack.

◊

Plopping his rump into the passenger-side seat, Jimmy glanced back at the silver, undulating wall. He could jump through right now; the clown was still making his way around to the opposite door. But . . . what would he be missing if he left now? The wall would be there. He could leave anytime.

Pogo climbed in through the driver's side and crouched in his own seat, his wig scrubbing away at a bare patch in the car's headliner. With shoulders hunched and knees bent to accom-modate his oversize shoes, he did not look comfortable. "Put your seat belt on, kid" he grumbled, unable to do the same without removing his puffy suit. "And don't gimmie any of that bad-role-model crap."

"Besides" he continued "I hardly ever drive this thing anywhere. Too dangerous: you never know when somebody is going to plant a car bomb or something."

Jimmy threw him a quizzical look.

"What? Oh . . . you've never seen this side of things, have you? To you, we're all happy-go-lucky buffoons, running around for your entertainment. You've never had to live in a world where you can't step safely outside your own home, for fear that one of your carrot-topped rivals will hurl something nasty and sharp into your cranium. Your people haven't seen what happens when the only jobs to be found are Across the Gap, and your own world slips into ruin. In your world . . . "

Jimmy was drumming on the dashboard with his hands; he had stopped listening.

"Right. What am I thinking? You're too young to worry about your own survival. Well, that will change. Here, have a peanut-butter sandwich." He handed one to Jimmy and chomped down on his own, suddenly ravenous as he turned the ignition and barreled out onto the street.

◊

Pogo swung the bug up onto the curb in front of Gags n' Gunpowder, causing his passenger to bounce in his seat as the vehicle's right side popped up on the sidewalk. He killed the engine. "C'mon, kid. We're going shopping."

Automatic door swung open for them, and they were greeted by their own images gazing down from a ceiling-mounted monitor and security camera. Red crosshairs overlaid the image, highlighting the point where the swiveling AK-47, mounted next to the camera, was aimed.

"Afternoon, Bernie!" Pogo waved at a wall of dark bulletproof glass in the front corner of the store. The machine gun swung gleefully up and down, returning his greeting.

The two of them walked along the aisles, the clown occasionally picking an item off of a nearby shelf to display it to Jimmy. "The finest in razor-wire yo-yos . . . just don't slip! If you let a finger touch its string, you've lost the point."

Jimmy lifted a radial arrangement of metal fans attached to a central ring, carefully avoiding the sharp outer edges. "Ah!" exclaimed Pogo. "A spinner. Put one of these on your unicycle, and it'll keep your enemies at a distance. But it will take you a while to get to that level; let's try something a little simpler. Explosive gum, maybe? Spike stilts— how good is you balance? Ah, here we go." He lifted a colorful multi-pointed jester hat. "The caltrop cap! Perfect."

He gave Jimmy a minute to examine the numerous metal tetrahedrons sewn loosely onto its surface, then placed the hat onto the boy's head, buckling the chin-strap tightly. "If you're running from someone and can't seem to shake them, just pluck one of those nasty-looking arrangements off of your hat and chuck it behind you. No matter how the thing falls, one point always sticks up, ready to impale your pursuant's foot. That will slow them down!"

In less than an hour, Pogo compiled a box of toys for the kid. "Don't worry about the expense" he said. "Consider it an advance; you'll earn easily enough to pay me back after your first show." He opened the door, motioning Jimmy in and plopping the box down in his lap. From the end of the block, an engine roared.

"Carrot-tops!" exclaimed the clown, spotting the van which was racing toward them. He leaped over the hood of the beetle with a deftness Jimmy would not have expected, slipping into the driver's seat with key in hand. He threw the bug into reverse, accelerating up onto the sidewalk.

The van shot past them, missing their front bumper by scant inches. As it zoomed by, an orange-wigged head poked up from its sunroof, followed quickly by a pair of hands holding a jug-gling club and a lighter. Pogo slammed his steering wheel over to one side as the flaming torch tumbled toward them; it bounced past their car and into the opening automatic doors of Gags 'n' Gunpowder.

"Oh, for Dog's sake!" screamed Pogo, gunning the engine. They shot off the sidewalk, directly across the street, and down an alleyway. Seconds later,

shock waves pummeled the back of the car as Gags n' Gunpowder exhaled flame, then busted its walls open as the store's contents went up in a final explosive sigh.

The end of the alleyway was coming up fast. Pogo stomped the brakes —there was no resistance. He pumped the break pedal. "Sneaky bastards!" he yelled, a look of genuine terror creeping over his face. He turned to look at Jimmy, eyes wide open, pupils dilated. "They cut the breaks!"

Jimmy wasted no time dumping the box of newly acquired gadgets onto the floor and unbuckling his seat belt. He took one look at the rapidly approaching brick wall, planted a foot on the dashboard, and launched himself into the undulating silver mess behind them.

◊

Jimmy clambered down from the Volks-wagen's front seat, kicking the door shut behind him and taking off at a sprint through the crowd. He dodged a stroller and neatly avoided a forgotten snow cone before colliding with a tent pole. His four-foot frame went down all at once, knees and skull planting into the dirt floor all at once. Tears came to his eyes, more from the shock than pain, as he lifted his grit-encrusted face from the earth.

Warm, familiar arms lifted him to his feet, and reflex took over. Jimmy clung tightly to his mother's waist.

"Oh my darling, where did you run off to! Another five minutes and I would have had the police in here searching for you." Her voice was stern but comforting. "Don't you ever run off without telling me where you're going, okay Jimmy? Please?" She reached for his face, tissue in hand to wipe away the dirt, but he buried his head into her side. She stroked his hair. "Shush, it's okay."

His cheeks stopped stinging after a few moments, and he turned sideways, still leaning against his mother but focused once again on the show. The troupe was finishing up with their famous twenty-man flaming torch juggle; together they kept sixty clubs aloft. The trick required intense concentration, but one clown glanced in Jimmy's direction and locked eyes with him. A cruel grin crept up the painted corners of his mouth.

A warm sense of kinship spread through Jimmy as he smiled back.

THE END

CLASH OF CULTURES

STEVE REDWOOD

The beggar got on Line One of the Madrid Metro at Cuatro Caminos. She was young, light-skinned, probably no more than twenty-five, wearing a long dirty dress that clung to her undernourished body like damp plastic film She was carrying a baby on one thin arm. The baby's face was half covered in blood, and a stream of snot dangled from its nose like a string of tiny pearls (rubies where the blood flecked them), proof that all that glisters is not necessarily gold.

An English couple, probably in their late thirties, both casually dressed in jeans and t-shirts, and both with that reddened blistered look suggesting unwary tourists who had shown too little respect for the Spanish sun, were sitting facing the doors, a large travelling bag between the man's feet. They stared horrified at the condition of the woman and the baby, but no one else seemed to take much notice. The elderly gentleman beside them quietly continued reading his bible, his lips moving unconsciously. The young man and woman in the seats directly opposite were tonguing each other's mouths like famished pangolins searching for ants, while the large well-dressed lady beside them, far too heavily made-up for a hot carriage, fanned herself furiously.

The young woman began her spiel the moment the train set off again.

"¡Una ayuda, por Dios! Soy una pobre madre que no tiene trabajo . . . "

The well-dressed lady glanced across and frowned, but no one else even looked up.

"But, Peter, the poor little mite's bleeding!" said the Englishwoman.

The elderly gentleman overheard. He had that special elegance that is sometimes seen in well-do-to men from the south, from Andalucía, perhaps, or Murcia, where even their complexions seem to exude a certain sandy richness.

"Pardon," he said, " you are English, no?"

"Yes," said the man, who was next to him. "We were wondering about that poor woman . . . surely the baby's very ill; it's bleeding terribly."

The man chuckled. "Oh, the appearances may deceive one. That is probably just paint or purée of tomato."

"What!"

"Yes, an old trick. This help the foolish hand towards the charitable pocket."

The couple looked across at the baby again. A viscous substance was now dribbling from its mouth, as if a group of avant-garde maggots were holding a conceptual art exhibition.

"Oh my god, Peter, I do believe the baby's dying!"

The gentleman spoke in a slightly condescending tone.

"Excuse me that I say it you, but I believe the baby is in fact already dead, has, as we say in Spain, already stretched the leg. It is . . . how do you say . . . a stiff. Since maybe a week, a month, longer. A common trick, as I have said you. Since we get a socialist government, the decencies are no longer respected."

The English couple looked incredulous, which encouraged the Spanish gentleman to continue.

"Yes, the strangers find it hard to understand what is happen here. You will notice, all the beggars carry babies. Everyone is sorry for a baby, especially a sick baby, and give more generously. Spanish people we have the big hearts! So every beggar need baby! Sometimes the baby is live, that is true. But this is not possible the most of the time. And the live babies are more expensive than dead babies. Clothes and food and napkins for the little bum. So they keep dead babies in big communal refrigerator in night—they pay friends in meat market with sex—and bring out of refrigerator every day. The baby then appear to change of colour and die in front of the travellers, and the shock contribute to induce big generousness."

The English couple stared at him, mouths open. He shook his head sadly.

"They do this especially in the touristical area of the Prado Museum and the Retiro Park because they know the tourists are more gulliver than local people. But recently, they start on this Line too, because many visitors go to train station Chamartín."

At this point, the made-up lady, pressed by her cosmetics more pitilessly than ever Giles Corey was in the Salem witch trials, looked across and addressed the gentleman from behind her fan, which never ceased to move like the feathers of a sparrow having a dust bath. A short animated exchange ensued, the elderly gentleman nodding vigorously. He turned back to the English couple.

"The señora understand a little English, she say, but she is very timid to speak it. She say beggars especially big problem during the rushing hours. They use more room than real people, because the layer of dirtiness on their bodies—dried urines and sweats, pustules, scars, lice—make them bigger, like a coat. And the smell, the . . . the stinkiness, force one to maintain even more distance to protect the nose."

Despite a warning look from her companion, the Englishwoman protested:

"Well, that poor woman just looks small and sick and pitiful to me."

The gentleman shook his head at her innocence.

"Exactly! That is the intention! She is a hardening case. You are visitors to our country, and very welcome too. The President Blayeer and the President Boosh are good men, although they put the foot a bit in Iraq, and it has turned out rather frog. But look the manner she is standing, not holding the support bars. Like a seaman in boat. Perfect balance. A lot of practice, no? This maybe her ten or eleven baby."

"Tenth or eleventh baby!"

"Sí sí Señora. That is how bad it is. They have babies more quick than the rabbits. Soon there are no Madrid people left in Madrid. And they take babies of friends to bring on the metro, so the friends can go on holidays to the beach and pass them bomba drinking and selling drugs while we are all work hard."

"But you just said . . . "

The Englishman nudged the woman, and coughed loudly to drown what she was saying.

"¡Una ayuda, por Dios!" whined the beggar. "Por la Virgen María,¡piedad! Mi pequeña está muy malita."

"What is she saying?" asked the Englishman, perhaps to placate the Spanish gentleman for his companion's obvious scepticism.

"She call Virgin Mary as if Virgin Mary have nothing to do all day, and she say her baby is very sick. This is usual. She can not confess the baby yet is dead, because if the baby is dead she can not ask for money to feed it, no? Soon she pretend it die, you will see."

"But I'm sure I just saw the baby move!" exclaimed the Englishwoman, clutching her companion's arm.

The Spanish gentleman smiled indulgently.

"I not doubt it, Señora. It is part of the trick. She push with secret stick or string. Sometimes she use vibrator, so people see she not use hands."

Before the tourists could reply to these astonishing revelations, the Max Factor female equivalent of the Man in the Iron Mask opposite burst into a new cascade of sound. She only finally came to a stop when a chunk of dried face cream broke off, and she herself broke off too, in order to repair the breach.

The pangolins continued to forage for saliva.

"The señora was remarking," said the gentleman, "that it is not just here in the cities that the situation is go out of control. You can not go to swimming in the Islands Canaries now, especially Fuerteventura and Gran Canaria, without bump into the bodies of boat people who are floating there. Like the bellyfishes.. I want to say, jellyfishes. Canoes, rowing boats, lunches, dingoes, cayucos—they will use anything to try reach the islands. I replied her that this drowning at least reduce a little the number of immigrants who are reach here and travelling free on the metro all day and enjoying of our tapas, but she say if they will insist on to drown, why they not do it nearer Marruecas or Mauritania or Senegal?"

"But that poor woman's just as white as me—or you," objected the Englishwoman.

"So much less excuse for her," replied the gentleman tranquilly. "One expect Africans and Arabics to be a trouble, it is in their nature, a shepherd not change his spots, but when white people start doing it too, it is the straw at the end!"

Just then they came into a station, and three Peruvian musicians got on, squat rotund creatures with cheerful smiles breaking through the jagged lava of their complexions. They accidentally knocked the beggar woman to one side, causing her to drop the baby.

"¡Y ahora un poco de música!" said the squattest, as he strummed a few notes on an old guitar, while a companion raised his pipes to his wrasse-like lips, and the third, a teenage girl, gazed around, wire-cutting eyes seeking out potential weak links in the chain of seated passengers. The guitarist unconsciously rested one foot on the baby, and broke into a rousing version of Cuando Llora Mi Guitarra. His face was so animated, it took topological possibilities to their limits.

The beggar woman made feeble attempts to rescue the baby from under the musician's foot, but her efforts were too weak to have any effect. The

Englishwoman started to rise to help the beggar, but her companion gently held her back, whispering, "Wait, we're foreigners here, best not to interfere yet."

The Peruvian girl traversed the three interlocking carriages with a small collecting pouch, ready to detect the most furtive of glances, the reckless exploratory lifting of a single eyebrow even, but faces were turned down and credit cards and fans clutched with bellicose determination.

It being impossible for the conversation to continue with such enthusiastic music, the Spanish gentleman had returned to reading his bible. The Englishman glanced at him, started, frowned, looked across at the beggar, then back at the gentleman, and then said something to his companion. She followed his example, and then nodded, clutching his arm tightly. They whispered excitedly.

When the next stop came, those who were getting off, eyes still averted, carefully chose the doors away from the musicians and the beggar. The singer gave a pointed and very loud "Gracias, sois muy amables", and the trio got off and dashed to the next carriage. They were replaced by a noisy group of students, all clutching their look-alike elastic-bound files and garishly coloured mobile phones, and a blind lady and her guide dog, a big Yellow Labrador.

The beggar was at last able to retrieve her baby, which she held close to her chest, seemingly unaware that her dress had fallen open, revealing one of her breasts. From its size, and colour of the nipple, it was clear she was lactating.

The Spanish gentleman must have spotted the Englishwoman's expression.

"There, you see!" he said. "These creatures have more tricks than ticks." He paused, as he became aware of his unintentional linguistic achievement. "More tricks than ticks," he repeated. His hot Iberian creative juices spurted again. "Indeed, more vices than lices, I may say! You are observing her breast. I know what you are thinking. But you are tourist and innocent, and can to be easily misleaded. They put rats on breast at night to make the milk to flow. That is why the rats in Madrid are so strong and healthy. They are like . . . how do you say? . . . humid nurses in the old times. Like your Jane Owsten. This give the impression that their baby have recently been sucking breast, so no one suspect baby is really dead since a long time."

The English couple were prevented from reacting to this intriguing information by the actions of the blind lady's dog. It either hadn't been all that well trained, or it hadn't been fed in the last day or two, for it growled ferociously and jumped up at the baby. The beggar only just managed to pull it away in time, but the dog kept on trying.

"¡Mira lo que hace tu maldito perro!" shouted one of the students in warning.

The blind lady compressed her lips tightly: she'd obviously been told by too many young jokesters to 'look' at her dog.

Having done her bit, the student shrugged and returned to recounting to her friends her adventures with a famous Brazilian footballer in a disco the night before. The Englishwoman shouted, "But it's ruining the baby!" and this time did actually rise and try to intervene, but the dog gave her a warning snap, and she hurriedly sat down again.

The noise finally disturbed the pangolins' feeding frenzy, and they looked up, dazed, their exhausted tongues lolling out of their mouths, the studs gleaming. They lovingly began to apply lip salve to each other.

"You see the trouble the beggar is cause!" the Spanish gentleman muttered with a heavy sigh, as the guide dog leapt up again, almost yanking the blind lady off her feet. "I hope you not judge our beautiful capital by such elements. Where are you alighting?"

"Plaza de . . . de Castilla," answered the Englishman. His mind was clearly on something else.

"Ah, Plaza de Castilla. There is not really much to see there—las Torres de Europa, maybe; though I fear me that our own Twin Towers are so small the terroristas could not find them, so they land at the airport and asked political asylum instead. When they were refused—we had a good Conservative government then under the Mister Aznar—they put the bombs on trains; that show you how are these people!"

"We're not stopping there, just changing lines." The Englishman hesitated, but obeying a nudge from his wife, added:

"Please don't take offence at this, but my wife and I couldn't help noticing . . . . well, it's really quite amazing how much she resembles you."

"Who?"

"The beggar."

The gentleman smiled.

"Actually, do you know, I was think the same. It occur to me she might to be my daughter. I can not say for sureness. She went away from home at a very short age. She not like the discipline. I often asked myself how she might look without the . . . the . . . the acme."

"Acne."

"Yes, I mean acne." Slightly offended at being corrected, the gentleman took off his glasses and began to clean them as the couple stared at him.

At this point, the guide dog finally succeeded in forcing the beggar to drop the baby again, and it at once began to savage it. It ripped through its clothes, revealing it to be a girl, and succeeded in biting off a leg. This seemed to satisfy its hunger, for it then began to lick with great enthusiasm between her buttocks.

"It is an interesting fact that the most of people not realise," said the old gentleman, replacing his glasses, "but the dogs are loving the human faeces. Protein, you know, and they say a probiotic too. In parts of India, I have read, dogs follow the naked children around waiting them to drop the shit."

"But if the beggar lady is your daughter . . . ," said the Englishman hesitantly, "that poor baby . . . "

" . . . might to be my granddaughter. I know. The life is full of surprises. The ways of God are indeed strange and wonderful, you not think? But we must not to

117

question His purpose." He sighed with a certain satisfaction. "It is a good thing she left home. I mean, look what she has resulted to be."

The made-up lady opposite, now secure behind her newly solidified crenellations, rejoined the conversation. The old gentleman listened with his usual politeness.

"The señora say that I am acting very bravely. That it is such disappointment when children result so badly. That is true. Sometimes one feel like blaming oneself, however illogical that might be. My own daughter a beggar! The shame is so great!"

"This man—these people—are disgusting!" whispered the Englishwoman to her companion, unable to contain her rising anger any longer. "Savages!"

"Shh. He might hear you. Anyway, remember this is a foreign country, and we must keep open minds. They just have different customs and moral values, that's all. They never had the advantage of the Reformation. Torquemada dies hard. Opus Dei rules."

"I don't care about different customs! Does that make treating poor people so badly all right? Or bull-fighting? Or bear-baiting? Or stringing up old greyhounds?"

"I think you're mistaken about the bear-baiting. Why, the bear and the strawberry tree are the symbols of Madrid. Don't you remember them from Sol? But this isn't the place to argue. With a bit of luck . . . "

She looked at him questioningly, then slowly smiled.

"Of course, why didn't I think of it before!"

He kissed her warmly on the cheek, and squeezed her hand. They said no more, but watched the guide dog cleaning the baby.

By an unfortunate chance, at the next stop two Metro guards got on, leading a muzzled German Shepherd.

Foolishly forgetting the rather serious handicap of the muzzle, the guard dog at once attacked the guide dog with gusto and claws. Newly nourished on the baby's leg, the latter fought back. The students shouted, the made-up lady dropped her compact case, the pangolins nibbled each other's noses, the beggar screamed, and the baby was lost somewhere among the canine limbs.

"This is new system on Madrid Metro," explained the Spanish gentleman, quite unruffled. "Just a few months. Like Paris, I believe. The dogs make turns of eight hours, and that may to be why the metro dog is a bit bad-mooded, if it has been working much hours. At the moment, the dogs are only on some of the lines . . . "

He stopped as he realised that he had lost his audience. The English couple had apparently been able to take no more, and were plunging through the mêlée trying to reach the doors.

"No be afraid!" he shouted, but the pair had already managed to leave the carriage and the mayhem within. "Have a good holiday in Madrid!" he shouted at the doors as they closed. "And no forget to try our famous tapas!"

◊

The English couple were back in their hotel room, both in an excellent mood. The man ate a sandwich they had bought on the way, the woman looking at it longingly, but refusing to spoil her appetite. They took a long time over their shower together, savouring what was to come afterwards. Then, still naked, almost shivering with anticipation, they filled the bath with fresh hot water, opened their travel bag and took out the dead baby that they had grabbed during all the confusion on the metro. Holding it by the one remaining leg, they gently put it in the steaming water. The woman washed it lovingly and thoroughly, while the man crouched down behind her, nibbling at her neck and caressing her breasts. They then dried it thoroughly, and took it into the bedroom.

"Let's do it together this time!" whispered the woman, her eyes shining, her hands clutched convulsively between her thighs.

The man stroked her hair fondly with one hand, his already erect penis with the other.

"That might be a bit difficult . . . "

"No, not if she's on top of you, and I kneel over you facing you. You can do your thing while I eat the buttocks."

"But we tried something like that once before, in Paris, remember, and you got so carried away you nearly bit my cock off by mistake!"

"Don't say you didn't enjoy it!"

"Well, yes, but it hurt like hell all the same. Jesus!"

"I'll be careful, I promise. Trust me, my sweet."

The man kissed her tenderly and lay down holding the tiny corpse over his groin, while his wife knelt down between his feet. They looked deep into each other's eyes.

"You know," said the man, his voice trembling a little with emotion, "if ever a marriage were made in Heaven . . . Can I make a confession?"

"What is it, dearest?"

"I never did like the killing part."

"I know, my darling. You're just too sweet. Don't think I don't appreciate your sacrifice, the way you gave up grave-robbing, and took to killing, just to make sure my food was fresh. But I think we have at last found an answer. We never need to harm any dear innocent little children again. We'll travel the metro, and only take babies who have just died. I wouldn't want to bump into that heartless Spanish man again, though."

"I know. What a cruel perverted bastard he was! His own daughter! And a blatant liar too: this baby was certainly still alive when the mother brought it on the train."

"I should hope so too! You know how delicate my stomach is."

After that, the only sounds in the hotel room for a long long time were those of pure innocent pleasure.

THE END

FREE CHOICE

DAVE MIGMAN

Geordie had a knife in his han
and the other bunched fine
Gis a fucken beer ya bas
Cut ya face
Cut a cunt in ya face

So it goes. Some bake serene
on beaches of silt or ash
others propagate the fear

They are pouring the little fish
packed with ice to freeze
down the little alley of night

And brawny old men plough sunset
fields with quiver flanked donkeys:
our narratives are self controlled
we can move or sink our teeth
we can choke on the blood of the past
regurgitate each savoured hellish moment
or we can burn the bridge
and alter the course.

IT'S FEAR

DAVE MIGMAN

Fear of failure
fear of my body
of touching and no longer feeling
as if the tips were made of stone
cold as the mountain.

Fear of rejection
fear of contagion
of hurting and hurt
of stricken words in evening
from mouth to mouth
a game of hurt

Fear
of rising then falling

Fear of the embrace tumbling full nelson
a lover's touch a lash of acid
Deceived by powders, unctions
my own foolish crown
my own desperation
seeking salvation

POLLUTO.

finding nothing but emptiness

It is this I fear

as I melt into the shadow
tail tucked between my legs.

MAGNET DRAGGED IT

DAVE MIGMAN

Piston march the mountain two hounds
to track the flies that linger in his
shadow. Flames curling
beneath the flesh. Clench. Unclench,
clench, eyes fixed on a specific
location beyond the stone, beyond the
sickle of the path.

The beast rose in his throat again,
a low growl. The dog stopped, poised
one paw raised, sniffed the air then
continued. He thought: I was nearly
there, as I moved through, village
to town city to mountain I evaded
it. But here too it has found me:

the shadow of the dual mind
—necessity of mans' fool mind

CIRCLE AND DJINN

ROBERT LAMB

The doctor lowered his slender, brass telescope. Perception swelled. The view of a primordial campfire expanded into the vastness of uncivilized wilderness. The flames became a distant pinpoint of flickering luminescence.

He stood at the edge of the cliff, his pale visage gleaming in the moonlight. The wind buffed him continuously, whipping his black cloak around him like the wings of things dying in a maelstrom. His face, while still regal and handsome, wore the aged lines of a life spent in the deep contemplation of lamentable paths. An eternal frown. Yet even such a seemingly unflinching mask still sparked with occasional darker humor.

Even now, staring off across the wild expanse of pitted forest beneath him, his thin lips curled into a faint smirk. He raised his arm and gestured toward the distant campfire at the base of the opposite canyon wall.

"There," he said to the deformed man at his side, "The primitives camp outside their warren of caves. They scrape hides from rib with sharpened stone, wrench viscera from dripping cavity and hang strips of muscle to roast above their ancient flame."

With this, he turned to his companion, looked into a face half-consumed by the still meat of palsy. The hunchback's body was just as twisted, every limb and protrusion malformed, emanating from a racked and crooked

125

spine. Yet Todor's one good eye and slack-jawed expression conveyed absolute devotion. Fear and awe.

I am God to him, the doctor thought.

"Are they that different from me?" he asked the twisted man. "They break down the form into its mere components. A string of gut becomes lace. Bones and antlers find new life as tools and trinkets. Each kill permits their continued existence—sustains them in the same way that their gathered firewood feeds a flame they could never hope to reignite. The spark was likely lighting-sent, ages ago, a gift from the Heavens in time out of mind. Tell me, am I so different?"

"I don't know," Todor grated, too terrified to dare apply even his own dim reasoning to such a quandary.

"My work is but the reverse," the doctor continued, looking hard at the hunchback. "I attempt to compile a thousand details and make something greater than the sum of its parts—and in doing so, shape the very future of man."

Todor trembled and averted his eye from his master. The doctor glanced at the distance beneath them, the treetops far beneath them in the valley.

The hunchback would jump if I commanded him, he realized, and was suddenly overcome by the thought.

The doctor parted his lips, raised his tongue to speak the killing words, but then relented. He turned his mind back to the work at hand: the overarching plan, the inevitable reunion.

"If I succeed," the doctor said, "my progeny and their decedents will stand as far from me as I stand from those cave dwellers."

He stared at the light of the distant camp. They had been there since the dawn, cut off in their deep canyon from the trials that had tested the rest of their kind. Undiscovered by the great migrations of man, they thrived not unlike the lemurs of Madagascar— unsuitable for the outside world, frozen in evolutionary stagnation.

Their time neared, however. Technology advanced too swiftly and humans grew too numerous. He had been lucky enough to hear rumors of the place. A British archeologist had published a controversial study on bones from the region, and local tales of ogres and trolls further collaborated the doctor's own private theories. He'd secured land on the very edge of gulf and moved most of his operations to an old manor house near by.

He'd dared venture into their domain only once, uncoiling the rope ladder from its great spool and climbing precariously through the tree tops. The descent alone had been treacherous enough for a man of his age, but upon reaching the ground, he'd felt an even greater danger bloom all around him.

Immersed in that canopied murk, his pistol had felt small in his hand, like a religious talisman rendered moot in a heathen land. After all, he had ventured into a great pit of years, where modernity felt more exposed than protected by its advancements. But his luck had held. He'd encountered only tracks during his descent. He'd spotted a single bone talisman dangling from a tree branch and even that had been enough to stir a long submerged terror.

What had he been thinking?

For the doctor was a man largely without fear—of neither the government whose laws he broke nor the god whose creation he manipulated. Even the inevitability of death failed to stir him. After all, he knew his likely murderer all too well. That lone traveler even now continued to work his way back from the desolate Arctic wastes.

No, all these fears were very much a part of his time, all corners of a fate he'd willingly carved out for himself. But he did not belong in the valley, and the ways of its people were not an ocean that a modern, learned man could hope to navigate.

He'd taken to spying on them through the telescope when they were in the clear. By this, he had learned much of their ways, of the conflicting energies that kept them frozen in time. On one count, they possessed a brutal determination. The were slaves to their desires, yet gave their lives over entirely to unflinching tradition. They lived the same day over and over again. To do different was anathema. They lived something of the animal life and something of the circular, in which each act means nothing unless it recreates something of the past. Even if he walked into their presence in the golden splendor of a God, what could they do but murder him and cast him like fuel upon the flames of their hunger?

Though perhaps my son . . .

No, they'd raise arms even against such a towering superior—in the same way they'd smash Todor's malformed skull beneath their stone age hammers.

The gulf between the two worlds spanned epochs.

"Master . . . do we . . . do we descend?" the hunchback stammered.

"No," the doctor said. "I've seen all I need to see."

◊

Once more into the laboratory, once more into the labyrinth of tubes and coiling brass that filled the sellers beneath the ancient manor.

The doctor walked slowly through the womb he'd crafted. Amber liquids gurgled through spiral pathways overhead, blood pumped through veins of glass, illuminated to ruby brilliance by soft, electric lighting. Still other contraptions surged with organic rhythm, laboring to maintain the proper mixtures, temperatures and sanguine tides. Steam seeped from copper valves, water gurgled from spigots to feed grated drains in the stone floor.

Moist warmth hung heavy in the air. Even now, the doctor ran a hand through his white hair and flicked sweat haphazardly to the side side. The place held the same temperature as any orifice, any wound.

At last he made his way to the center of the work and stood before the great cylindrical vat. A pale form floated in the dark, embryonic fluid, trailing tubes towards the capping, conical lid. It hummed, ever so slightly.

Years earlier, the apparatus had birthed this creature's tragic predecessor. She had been beautiful and strong of body, but fatally weak in spirit. How her screams still resonated through the worst of his nightmares.

Prior to that doomed daughter, these waters had housed his son—and countless failures before that: stillborn Adonises and shrieking things more wound than man.

Some had stepped forth from the vat seemingly perfect, eyes brimming with vital fire, muscles taunt with power —and then he'd watched in anguish as the patina of flesh ripped and slipped from them like the skin of a rotten fruit. Screaming with lipless mouths, lidless eyes wide with agony, they'd walked over piles of cancer-black viscera as it continued to spill from their abdomens. With trembling fingers, they'd reached for the author of their agony, unable to speak the questions that welled up from their un-languaged hearts.

How many had he felled with his pistol during those dark years of trial and error? How many disappointments?

But this one—this daughter was different.

He placed his bare hand against the tank, swept enough condensation away to peer into its murky depths. Her chestnut hair drifted around her hidden face like seaweed. He could just make out the blissful curves of her pale thighs and full breasts.

An oxymoron: the mother in utero.

"Soon," he said. "Soon."

He felt his heart rise at the thought, even sensed a stirring in his loins. This was what it felt like, he realized, to stand at the end of era. Just as a machine may harness enormous energies and focus them through a single mechanical part, so too one man could become the fulcrum on which the world changed.

I am the fulcrum.

If his endless calculations were correct, then the disaster with the first daughter and the groom's estrangement would pay off. The son's journey home would be one of countless lessons.

Just as mine was.

Driven mad with grief, his prized creation had attempted to pay back all his pain in blood. He'd strangled the doctor's wife, burned his home and pursued him relentlessly to the very ends of the Earth. And there, in that frozen Cocytus, mere chance had robbed them both of their well-earned deaths.

The doctor winked sweat from his eyes. He'd spent the years since that encounter pondering his missteps. Freed from the demands of a normal, married life, he'd plotted the course that would set his Adam back on the golden path.

The only question was whether the son would murder him when he returned. It mattered little in the grand design. His role, like that of all grand-fathers, was merely to prepare the way.

He moved his hand from the glass surface of the vat, water dripping from his fingertips. Inside the tank, the woman stirred.

◊

Days become weeks and weeks months. The woman in the vat grew stronger, stirred more in prenatal dreams. The primitives in the sunken forest continued to feed their god-sent flames. They rutted in the dust and settled disputes with the brutal indifference of an eternally, looping past. He continued to postpone his plans to capture one for dissection. It was, after all, an unnecessarily dangerous side project.

Todor grew increasingly skittish. He stammered more in his addresses to his master, asked incessantly about their seclusion from the primitives.

"Their refuge is also their prison," the doctor would reply. "They live in a tidal pool of time."

Yet no answer would calm him. The hunchback continued to ask questions about sounds in the night. What he truly feared, the doctor knew, was the son's return. Incapable of comprehending the greater plan, Todor saw only apocalypse in the impending reunion.

For all his physical and spiritual ailments, however, the hunchback was a decent chef.

The doctor sat at the long table in the great dining room. Under the dead gazes of a dozen mounted elk heads, he nimbly sliced into the roasted duck. As always, he found his thoughts wandering. His mind on a distant future, his hands inevitably drifted back into well-worn patterns of vivisection. It wasn't till he reached for nonexistent forceps that he realized what he'd done. He looked down into the disassembled mallard: parted muscles, exposed bone and pink arteries. A hint of blood.

He took a sip of wine, had a bite of garlic potato instead. Glimpsing the blood again, he thought again of the first daughter—a glass vat behind her spiderwebbing with cracks, suddenly coated with the brain and bone-speckled gore of a cranial exit wound. He'd shot her through the eye.

He closed his eyes, forced it all away. His hunger waned.

He heard the sound of his misshapen servant moving in the nearby hall, floorboards creaking underneath his gait.

"You may have this bird," he called to the darkness beyond the light of the candelabra. "I fear you've undercooked it."

"May I?" replied a voice from the dark.

The doctor froze. Fork and knife clattered against his plate.

It was not Todor.

"What I would have given for such a meal in the frozen wastes," the voice said, at once refined and gravely. "For days, I ate nothing. I wandered frostbitten and starving. Then I happened upon a team of Dutch explorers as famished as me. They'd shot a polar bear and I joined them in their feast."

The doctor's heart quickened as he heard the footsteps grow closer, the figure still hidden in the room's outer dark.

"Did you know, father, that the liver of the polar bear is toxic?" The unseen man asked. "Too rich in vitamin A, you see—though we didn't know it at the time. Then the fevers came. Our visions blurred and we vomited our steaming meals back up on the snow. Our *skin* began to peal—can you imagine it? Poor Gaobert experienced the worst of it—the very soles of his feet came off. His face slid away from a new landscape of blister. He and Ebekin slipped into coma and never revived. Balderic and I, however, continued through the wastes in fevered delirium, our bandages frozen with gore, bundled against the hellish visions that pursued us."

He spoke as if these were but trivial things. There was detached amusement, but no hatred.

The figure stepped into the quivering candle light and the doctor gasped. "My son . . . "

He was dressed as a mere traveler, neither fancily nor impoverished. The mane of thick, black hair was gone, the scalp now hairless and twisted by scars. His face still held the same statuesque proportions, yet all was ravaged by frostbite and the unimaginable suffering of vitamin poisoning.

"I knew you'd survive," the doctor said, his fingers fidgeting uncontrollably around his plate. "I knew you'd return."

The son stepped up to the table and reached down for the doctor's plate. He placed one thumbless hand against the breast and ripped off a duck leg with the other, three-fingered hand.

"And you knew as well," the son said through a mouthful of meat, "that the journey would give me time to think, to process what had transpired between us—and you knew the treck home would change me more than the treck forth. Hmmm?"

"She was an unfit mate for you," he said.

The son nodded, staring off to one side into the dark. "Yes, I see that now."

"I have made another for you."

"I know you have, father. Take me to her."

◊

Father and son descended into the cellar, down the spiral stairs and into the midst of the divine forge.

So many frenzied hours had gone into its construction, so many precursory experiments. Early on, when the work demanded cadavers, he'd been fortunate enough to happen upon Todor. In the dark of night, they'd converged on the same grave, though for drastically different purposes. A mutually beneficial bargain was reached.

The hunchback, naturally, was absent. He'd feared his master's progeny from the start, though he feared most things with beating hearts and judging eyes.

The doctor led his son to the vat and watched as he swept away moisture with his large, disfigured hands. He stared in at his bride-to-be and a smile flashed across his scar-twisted lips.

"I would tell her much of love, father," he said. "And more of desire. I was slow in returning to you, I'll have you know, as my self-education proved a continued and necessary distraction. I encountered a great man in England—a man, like me, marked about the face by grievous scars—twin cheek wounds from a single Somali spear. Most men of this world sleep, but this adventurer was very near awake, though afflicted like the rest of you with depressive spells and carnal lust. Even he was too distracted by the path he traveled to full navigate it. Yet he became my tutor for a month, in between his own adventures. He was amazed by how fast I learned. In addition to language, writing and philosophy, he told me all he knew of the flesh—the lessons he'd learned in the brothels of Karachi."

The son stared intently at the woman in the murk, emotion moment-arily flashing through his face.

"This one is strong," the doctor said.

"I know, father."

The son turned and the two men stared into each other's eyes, truly matching gazes for the first time since those final moments in that Arctic wasteland.

How that meeting had occupied his mind the last two years, looped repeatedly in his daily thoughts. Choking in the vice-like grip of his creation, he'd clawed at the iron-hard arms that held him, feet dangling, aloft. He'd stared into what was then still a beautiful count-enance, unmarked by the ravages of his return journey, though animated to such demonic anguish over lost love. -

And that howling, existential dilemma.

"Who am I, father?" he had gasped in clouds of misted breath, as their combined weight sent cracks across the thin shelf of ice beneath them. "I dare you. I dare you! Justify your ways to—"

And then the surface had broken, plunging the son into an icy chasm. Somehow, the father managed to catch himself, scramble and pull himself back up onto level wastes.

Looking into the man's destroyed face now, the doctor could tell that his progeny had found no answer to the question—and well that he hadn't. Such an unexpected surge of faith or righteousness might have doomed the golden path he'd foreseen. Instead, his Adam merely probed its untouchable depths as even the best of men must.

As quickly as it had occurred, the moment slipped away. The son glanced back the way they'd come. There was the sound of shrieking and crashing from up in the manor.

Guttural cries. Fear and rage.

Oh god . . .

"The primitives . . . " he gasped.

◊

The cave dwellers' ascension from the forest gulf was, of course, impossible. Their domain was their prison, locked eons ago by geological upheaval. There was only the rope ladder, and it was coiled at the cliff . . .

The doctor realized his miscalculation. The prodigal son had returned—and while he'd expected the hunchback to begrudge them both, he'd never imagined he'd stoop to such disastrous depths of treachery.

"He damns us all…" the doctor gasped.

But the son merely smiled and cast his eyes over at the nearby surgical theater—still prepared, ironically, for the vivisection of the primitive race that even now invaded the manor.

"Don't fret, father," he said, walking over to the table. He scanned the assembled surgical tools, moving an open hand over them as if to bless them in some arcane rite. At last, his right hand selected a long blade.

The doctor fretted that his pistol was still upstairs. After all, the one threat he'd anticipated in his own house stood beside him now. The one variable in the plan had always been whether his creation would still wish to murder him

Todor's betrayal, however . . .

He followed the hulking traveler up the spiral staircase, the sounds of breaking glass and howling echoes growing with each step. He had to lace his fingers to keep his hands from shaking, but the son walked with seamless calm, as if casually approaching a warm bath rather than the brute savagery of a bestial past.

They emerged into one of the long corridors, encountering nothing right away—but then the first of the brutes galloped around the corner. It stopped the moment it saw them, then screeched something unintelligible and two others quickly joined it.

They were but savage silhouettes in the faint lighting—all matted hair and gut-laced hides. Trinkets of bone clattered against them and each brandished a savage stone weapon.

Muscles tensed.

And then it happened.

The doctor gasped in awe at his creation's reflexes, clearly honed during his travels into something preternatural. He caught the wrist of the first attacker in mid hammer-swing, then buried the blade in the hairy cunt of the thing's armpit, spraying the floor beneath them in a fountain of blood.

The son shoved the dead thing writhing to the floor, weapon and all, then lunged to avoid a swooping axe. Its owner unbalanced by the momentum of its attack, the son sent the thing sprawling with a low kick. Before the attacker could rise to its feet again, the son scooped up the stone hammer and brought it down in a lethal arch, splitting skull and cracking teeth.

The remaining primitive now hesitated, uncertain of what strategy to employ. The thing stood in the light of a hallway lantern and the doctor read the loops of well-worn instinct in the face, the chains of unwavering tradition: fear, shock, rage at the unknown. A long ladder had descended from the cliffs and its universe had exploded to dimensions it could never hope to fathom.

It howled and ran at the doctor's god-like progeny. The son cast the hammer aside, caught the cave dweller's axe by the upper handle and head butted the thing in the face. It dropped its weapon, stumbled backwards with blood cascading from its ruined nose. Then, in a flash, the son scooped the axe up and brought it up in a rising, underhanded swing. It split jaw and throat, came to a stop somewhere in the sinuses. The thing collapsed in blood-sopped screams.

They stood there for but a moment, the stink of unwashed bodies and smoked hides mingling with that of blood and death-loosened bowels. Still trembling, the doctor felt the rough, damp hand on his shoulder.

"Come," he said. "There are more in the den."

◊

The son led them boldly through the darkened corridors, armed like one who walked betwixt the ages of man: stone axe in one fist, surgical blade gripped precariously in the other. He'd tucked one of the hammers into he belt.

They strolled through the ransacked dining room. The mounted animal heads had been hacked from the walls. The suit of armor lay in pieces on the carpet, glittering in the light of the curiously untouched candelabra.

They stepped into the great den and saw the remnants of the primitive raiding party. Some six bestial men—all hides, beard and tangled hair—gathered around the fiercely blazing hearth, ensorcelled by the raging fireplace.

The doctor gaped at the sight, his own terror momentarily forgotten. To the primitives, fire was divine—the inheritance of a previous age. To climb the ladder and discover a mansion containing such a furnace as this . . . it was a journey into the land of gods.

He scanned their number again and saw that there seemed a seventh as well—standing to the side, smaller than its peers but draped in wretched hides as well.

The son raised the stone axe above his head: a flash, a sudden flourish, and the axe flew across the room. One of the kneeling primitives howled, clawed at the handle now protruding from this back of its skull, then tumbled over face-first before the fire.

The others turned, saw, and rose in a torrent of bared teeth.

The doctor stood back, numb, and watched the son block one blow, then another. He buried the hammer into the skull of one attacker, ripped the very jawbone from the head of another. Blood sloshed soundlessly on the Persian rug, bodies fell in muffled heaps.

And then there was a gunshot.

A splitting pain.

The doctor looked down at his chest: black fabric soaked wet, a crimson stain seeping out through the white silk. He looked up and saw the hunchback, dressed in hides, wide-eyed and crazed.

Why?

Todor dropped the weapon from his shaking hand.

The doctor swooned, reached to brace himself against the back of an elegant reading chair—instead collapsed across it.

He strained his head to look up and saw the hunchback flee through a servant's door.

Meanwhile, the son had culled the number of assailants down to two, with whom he wrestled and brawled bare-handed. They bit into each other's flesh, clawed at eyes. Finally, the son ripped the throat from one with his bare teeth, spit the sopping meat to the floor and, on his knees, straddled the survivor. He leveled punch after punch into the thing's face, smashing cartilage, splintering bone into brain, spilling teeth and sloshing gouts of blood with each blow.

At some point, he stopped. He looked up from the strewn carnage all about him and gazed over at his father. The only sound was that of flickering flame, the hiss and pop of burning wood.

"Lessons, father," he said, his voice devoid of pity or concern. "A taste of the path ahead."

But the doctor couldn't speak. He watched his son rise, still bleeding from numerous wounds—half an ear lost in the final brawl.

He walked out of sight and, for a while, the dying father merely stared at the fire. He managed to work himself into a proper sitting position and thought again of Todor.

Why had the broken little man done it? Why had he dressed in hides and sought them out? He'd always seemed to loath or fear the company of anyone save the freshly dead. If he'd descended among the primitives, how had he even survived?

When the son returned, he was bearing the docile body of the woman from the vats. Her pale skin still dripped with embryonic fluid, her umbilical cords dangled like the lifeless tentacles of some creature dragged from the depths.

He laid her down in midst of the dead, on the bloody carpet, and then stripped, revealing more scars of the arctic peeling, all canvassed over perfect musculature—like mold growing on a marble statue. His member stood fully erect, gleaming in the light of the hearth —true Promethean fire that it was.

His vision blurring, the doctor watched as he joined her on the bloody floor. It felt as if he watched through the cheesecloth of dream. Steadily, she woke from stupor as he caressed her with rough hands, teased the cleft of her sex with the deftest of tongues. When he finally penetrated her, she cried aloud, grunting and panting with each thrust.

They rolled in the gore of history, glistened bloody in the fire light as they fucked their way through countless positions, endless carnal knots.

Their orgasms rose in waves, crashed in echoes against vaulted ceiling.

◊

He looked down at his dead father. He touched the old man's cold cheek with a mangled hand, leaving behind a bloody swath. He reflected on how much he'd once wanted to kill this man himself, though that now seemed another life entirely.

He'd read many marvels during his travels and now they flowed through him. He thought of myths and poetry, of the ancient tales that the scared Englishman had shared with him. He resisted the urge to do something overtly symbolic with his father's corpse.

He chuckled.

There would be time enough for crafting wonders from human thoughts and dreams—dear God, the monuments they would build and climb! While the doctor had dealt in flesh, his own pallet would be ideas.

He selected a splintered table leg and set it to the blazing hearth. Then he spread the fire to each of the room's tall curtains. He found the garments the doctor had evidently procured for his children and tucked them under his arm.

The man and woman walked out naked into the cold, steaming against the chill. They caught glimpse of fear-stricken creatures moving the brush, but paid them no heed.

They walked to the nearby stream and bathed in the chilling waters, scrubbing stains and cleansing wounds.

The woman said nothing, but he had himself uttered only a few words. Once his lectures began, he had no doubt she'd learn his languages as swiftly as he'd stolen them himself. He caught himself glancing again and again at her flat stomach. Somehow he knew she was already with child.

Our child.

They dried themselves in the growing warmth of the burning manor house. They dressed as denizens of a civilized age and took horses from the stables.

They rode near the forested gulf as they departed. The son spotted a rising column of campfire smoke form the forest and knew the tormented hunchback had retreated there. He'd rejoined the brutal women who loved him like some broken child—and perhaps husband now as well. He would leave them to their coupling.

He laughed as they rode, overcome again by symbolism, reminded of what the wounded adventurer had told him that first night as they sipped wine in a his sitting room.

"They believe the Djinn were creations of fire, and man of clay," Burton had said. "Interesting, isn't it? The one pliable, the other easily starved or snuffed."

"But who is the kiln, my friend?" the son had asked. "Who is the kiln?"

They rode for the sun-crested horizon, towards the golden promise of cities, science and dream.

THE END

SILENT TREATMENT

ERIK WILLIAMS

Sunday

It's hot this morning. Is there a heat wave passing through? It's only April. Sure, it can get hot in April but it's Sahara-hot. It feels like an oven in here.

"Gwen?"

Still asleep. And under the covers to boot.

Not like she'd talk to me anyway. I don't know what I did to piss Gwen off but I must have fucked up good. It feels like ages now since she's talked to me.

God it's hot.

The sheets stick to my skin as I climb out of bed. Gwen doesn't stir. Just keeps snoring like a bear hibernating in the middle of the Gobi desert.

It's that fucking hot. I mean it's the kind of hot that makes you want to quit living.

The windows are closed. The thermostat reads ninety.

Gwen likes to keep the house around seventy-five in the evenings. Lately, it's dropped to around sixty at night. But ninety? How the Hell had she managed that? Probably did it to piss me off.

"Damn it, Gwen, you cranked up the heat too high," I say.

No reply. Gwen's a master at ignoring me. The one talent God gave her she executes with a surgeon's precision, giving me the silent treatment every moment of the day lately.

I flick the heat over to a/c.

Gwen is still cocooned under the covers. Her internal thermometer tends to sit one hundred and eighty degrees out of phase with mine when she's feeling spiteful. If it's cold, she's hot. If it's hot, she's freezing.

Sometimes I wonder if she's got a medical condition. Maybe anemia. Maybe she's just fucking crazy.

"Wake up, Gwen."

No response. Like I said, Gwen is a ninja at giving the silent treatment.

For a while now, I've tried to talk to her but she acts like I don't exist. I try to touch her, she walks away, timing her movement perfectly so I always miss even slightly brushing her skin.

Jerking off sounds good. Maybe that'll get her attention, rouse her out of her slumber. Gwen used to get turned on watching me rub one out. Used to make her want it.

I sit on my side of the bed, focused on her ripe lips, stroking my rod. It doesn't work.

Other women flash through my mind, hotter chicks with better bodies and an undying desire to pay attention to me. They talk to me. My little soldier salutes.

Sweat's rolling down my back and collecting between my ass and the mattress. I'm sitting on a soaked sponge of my own juices.

It's too hot to jerk off. Whatever energy all those adoring women created disappears. My rod dies a natural death. Now I'm pissed.

"Wake up," I say.

Gwen stirs but doesn't wake up. She burrows deeper into the covers. She's trying to make me think she's actually cold. What a bitch.

Many might think our marriage is rocky. I'd probably agree, if I knew what had caused the rockiness in the first place. Gaining that little bit of knowledge would require Gwen to actually open her mouth and address me rather than her friends, the mailman, her cat, or even the television. I mean I love her, you know. It's not like I want to have marriage problems. It takes two to tango, though.

My body's covered with salt and sweat. The a/c will take a while to beat back this inferno. I think about kicking the bed, maybe even slapping Gwen's ass hard. That would get her attention.

I know better than to force her to speak, though. Trying to compel Gwen to break her code of silence only prolongs the silence.

It's too hot to argue. Gwen can have her silent oven.

A cold shower and some time in the basement awaits.

Monday

Gwen invites a bunch of her snobby friends over for wine and cheese. Does she tell me? Of course not. That would require talking to me.

I emerge from my basement office after a full day's work writing nothing to find my living room filled with all the sorts of people I hate.

Gwen attracts people I hate with special pheromones used just to piss me off. It's true. How's that for spite?

No one seems to notice me. I walk around the room, looking people over, trying to act polite. Not one says a damn thing in return.

"Good evening," I say.

Stone faced.

I hate Gwen's friends.

"How's the wine?" I say.

Slurp. No response.

I'd shove the wine bottle up his ass but am afraid he'd enjoy it and the party would descend into a kind of Roman wine bottle penetration orgy.

Gwen's still performing wonderfully at ignoring me. She chats with some guy, sipping merlot, laughing at stupid jokes.

I stand next to her. She keeps talking.

God she's good. Even the guy talking to her is in on it, pretending like I'm not there. Hell, she's got everyone in on it.

Fuck her. Fuck her friends.

Walking by a bottle of wine, I knock it over, watching it shatter Shiraz all over the bamboo floors. Several people jump. One girl yelps.

None look at me, though. They're all focused on the shattered bottle.

"Don't worry," Gwen says. "Probably just the cat."

The cat. The cat gets more acknowledgement than I do.

I head back to the basement.

Tuesday

Another day of sitting in the basement with nothing to show for it. No new ideas. No inspiration.

I blame Gwen. Her performance last night only added to my growing frustration. What the hell pissed her off so much? Concentration on anything evades me like a girl in high school.

Thank God for the internet. No inspiration, no problem. Just find a few quality porn sites and let the time melt away.

Can't distract me from that, Gwen.

So many hot girls, looking at the camera, looking at me. Wanting me.

"Hey, Jill." I don't know her real name but Jill's good enough. "You look nice with your ass up in the air like that. Would you like to discuss the importance of global free trade?"

Why yes, I would.

My rod swells to mythic proportions.

Fuck my hands are cold.

It takes me a few minutes to dig a ski glove out of a storage bin.

My rod's still going strong. Jill still has her ass in the air and is interested in hearing my opinion on China devaluing its currency.

It feels like I'm getting a hand job from a snow bunny.

I'm looking at Jill. We're discussing cotton futures. I'm ready to shoot my wad.

Gwen's fucking cat jumps on the desk. It arches its back and hisses at me. Fucking Gwen.

The cat must have hit a button on the keyboard because Jill is gone. My erection follows.

The cat must have a psychic link with Gwen. It probably told her I was enjoying a riveting conversation with Jill.

Can't have that.

Gwen's agent, the cat, curls up on the desk and stares at me.

Fucking Gwen and her fucking cat.

Where is Gwen anyway?

Well after midnight. Probably out with her asshole friends. As long as she doesn't bring them back here.

Will you stop staring at me?

Wednesday

Another wasted day. Didn't even have the motivation to look at porn.

It's a bad day when you don't have the energy for porn.

Gwen's still gone. Don't think she's been back since yesterday. Probably got sloppy drunk and passed out on a friend's couch last night.

It's almost midnight. Staying away makes it easier for Gwen to ignore me. How convenient.

The door to the house opens. I hear footsteps above me. I hear giggles. I hear a man chuckling.

Damn it, Gwen brought one of her asshole friends over.

POLLUTO.

I emerge from the basement to find the guy from two nights ago, the guy who ignored me with Gwen, buried between my wife's legs.

"Do it like last night, baby," Gwen says. Her back arches her chest toward the ceiling.

Now most people might think we have a rocky marriage. At this point, I must agree.

"What the Hell are you doing?"

I stand next to the couch, looking down into Gwen's flushed red face. She moans loud. Probably so she can block out my voice.

Fucking bitch. I mean, I love her and all that but the thought of killing her runs through my mind. Her and this dick head.

It's one thing to ignore me. It's another to fuck some asshole in front of your husband.

The guy goes to town. Gwen rubs her breasts. Slurping sounds echo off the bamboo floors.

My blood boils. My fists clench. I'm ready for action. I'm ready to kill.

The cat beats me to it. It jumps on the guys head. The cat digs its claws into flesh, arches its back, and hisses at me.

The guy fucking freaks. He jumps up from Gwen's snatch, screaming and turning in circles.

The cat digs in more, keeping itself from flying off.

The guy screams louder. He runs around the room, begging for help.

I laugh my ass off.

Gwen rushes to his side; skirt still hiked up over her naked ass, and coaxes the cat off his head.

I can't stop laughing.

Blood runs down the guy's face in little streams. The cat sits in Gwen's arms, still staring at me.

Gwen's agent turned double agent.

"I'm out of here," the guy says.

"Come on, let me help you clean it up," Gwen says.

The guy shakes his head and leaves.

A smile of triumph finds a prominent residence on my face.

"I think we should talk about this."

But Gwen doesn't even look at me. She drops the cat and heads toward the bedroom, her skirt still hiked over her ass.

"Why don't you fix your skirt at least?"

Gwen ignores me. What a surprise.

The idea of killing my self crosses my mind. Then I realize that would be the ultimate concession of defeat. Fuck that. I won't give Gwen the satisfaction of offing myself.

Thursday

Fuck it's hot.

Gwen has the heat blasting again. She's already up, in the shower.

I get up and walk into the bathroom, sweat oozing out of my pores.

The bathroom is a steam bath.

"Gwen, what's with the heat?"

No response.

Fuck this bitch. She wants to ignore me?

I get in the shower. Gwen's full figure is turned away from me, giving me the money shot of her fantastic ass.

My rod says, "Good morning."

I don't hesitate. I start pumping.

Gwen can ignore me. She can fuck other guys. She can even pretend I don't exist. But I will get her to acknowledge me.

The water is hot. The steam is hot. I have about an ounce of water left in me. But I don't stop. I won't let Gwen win.

Gwen turns around and looks right at me. I keep pumping.

"I'm going to shoot all over you, bitch."

144

Gwen rinses her hair.

"I'm not kidding."

Gwen shuts the water off, grabs her towel and gets out.

I'm left standing in the shower, dripping, sweating, and holding my flaccid dick in my hand.

Gwen wins again.

I think of quitting all together. An image of a noose dances around my mind. Let Gwen find me hanging.

But she'd probably see it as the ultimate sign of victory. Probably would invite all her asshole friends over to view my swinging body.

I get out of the shower. Gwen stands in front of the sink running the towel through her hair.

Her mastery of the silent treatment is truly remarkable. I can't help but respect it.

I don't say anything else. Instead, I take my finger and write words into the fogged-over mirror.

Gwen stares as I write, "Talk to me."

Finally, I get a reaction. Although I don't know why she would stare. It's a pretty simple request.

Just when I think I've broken through her wall of silence, Gwen flees from the bathroom. Guess a stare is all I'll get today.

Friday

Gwen brings her asshole friends over again. But this time they don't drink wine and chat. They light candles and sit around a table.

Like I said, Gwen collects friends she knows I'll hate.

Some old bag sits in the middle. They hold hands and chant gibberish.

I stand in the corner, watching. No one says a damn thing to me. All on the same page as Gwen.

Fucking Gwen.

"Is Randy there?" the old woman says.

Is this a joke?

"Yes, I'm right here," I say.

"He says he's here," the old woman tells everyone else around the table.

They all nod excitedly.

What the fuck?

I swear Gwen knows no bounds. She gets all these assholes to ignore me except the old woman, who acts like she's the only one who can hear me.

"Yeah, I'm here," I say. "I'm always here. Can we stop playing games?"

The old woman repeats what I say. Everyone seems nervous.

"What games?" the old woman asks.

"Why Gwen blasts the heat? Why she fucks some guy in front of me? Why she ignores me while I jerk off?"

The old woman doesn't repeat any of this.

"Why doesn't she talk to me?" I yell.

The old woman repeats this.

A few moments later, the old woman says, "Randy, you're dead. You killed yourself a year ago."

Gwen wins again.

Saturday

So I'm dead. Apparently, I killed myself a year ago. Hanged myself in the basement.

This all came out at the séance last night. Gwen said she found me down there. Told me I'd been depressed for months, unable to write, unable to perform sexually.

The old woman told me the dead don't always realize they're dead. That's why everything seemed real to me.

Bullshit. Sounds like the worn out plot of ghost story written by an Indian guy with a fear of water. Gwen is full of it if she thinks I'm going to buy that crap.

146

How low do you have to be to try and convince your significant other they're dead?

Fucking bitch.

Like I'd ever kill myself. Or ever had problems with sex. I'm the fucking macdaddy when it comes to sex. Just have had a problem rubbing one out lately. But I think I've got a good excuse for that: Gwen.

I told the old lady to stick it up her ass last night. That didn't go over too well. Gwen packed up her bags and left. Didn't say one word to me on the way out. Silent treatment to the very end.

One Week Later

Gwen stopped by today. I didn't even try to talk to her. I've decided to fight fire with fire. I'm now giving her the silent treatment.

She left a picture for me on the kitchen table and departed almost as soon as she walked in.

The picture shows Gwen standing next to a tombstone with my name on it.

The woman knows no bounds.

I think about the noose again but chase it away. Gwen is a tough opponent but I won't give up. I'll win.

Just have to be patient. Porn will help. Maybe Jill will want to talk about the rising value of zinc.

Two Weeks Later

I'm not dead. Everyone thinks I am but I'm not.

Would call family but all I have...correction, I had was Gwen.

Gwen.

Gwen who swears I'm dead. Other people see me, though. I force them to acknowledge me. Outside, they walk around with their mouths open, looking at the ground or the sky with their Ipods playing music, allowing them to tune out the world and cocoon themselves in self-loathing.

I stop them. I interrupt there methadone dazes. I jump in their faces and scream "I'm not dead!" or "Fuck Gwen!" Then they shriek and run away.

Gwen would say they shriek and run because I'm a ghost manifesting itself or some bullshit like that.

I'm alive, baby. And I can prove it.

Sitting at the kitchen table, I lay my left hand across the cutting board and lift the cleaver with my right.

"I'm not dead," I say. "If I am, this won't do anything."

I hesitate. I'm not dead, I know. And in that case, this will hurt like a sonofabitch. But I have to prove it, have to show Gwen I'm still here. Still her husband. Still alive.

Swing the cleaver down in one fast movement.

Fuuuuccccckkkk!

Collapse to the floor, cradling my left stump to my chest, swearing and blinking the spraying blood out of my eyes.

Not dead.

Smile. Fuck Gwen. Knew it.

Two Hours Later

Blink. Hear something.

Door?

Footsteps.

Blink more. Cold. Weak.

"Finally." Gwen's voice. Far away. Like underwater.

Footsteps.

"About time." Gwen. Voice underwater. Slow-motion.

Door closes.

She acknowledged me. Not dead.

POLLUTO.

Ha! Told you so.

Cold. Shiver. Feel empty.

THE END

SANDY STRAVINSKY'S BEST DATE EVER

WILLIAM PEACOCK

Sandy didn't know what to think, where to go, what to make of herself. Her thesis on the cathartic and life-affirming thrill of jet cockpit out-of-body experiences had not only failed to impress her instructors, but had made her expulsion from aviation school an inevitability. Looking on the bright side, however, she had to admit that the accompanying notoriety was no doubt what had landed her tonight's big date with dreamy fellow cadet Ace Rogers.

Waiting for him outside the Museum of Art, where they'd agreed to rendezvous, Sandy was all irresistibly reptilian ersatz bohemia in a low-cut snakeskin rhinestone jumpsuit with crossbones brooch and fedora with alligator tooth hatband.

"Who needs flight school anyway?" she asked herself.

Now she was *really* flying high, higher than the time she had gone up in the B-52 over Cambodian airspace with a tank full of nitrous oxide.

She snapped out her compact to inspect herself.

"Why do you look so worried? You'll do fine, I promise. As long as you keep your big mouth shut and don't scare him off like that last guy, Heinrich. And the guy before that, and the guy before that, and the guy before that, and the guy before that, the one with the bungalow in Brazil. What was his name? Adolf? He was nice, Sandy, you two could have been happy together, I know it, but you had to go and botch it up and ruin everything by blabbing every detail of your sordid life to him, didn't you? Didn't you!"

But just then she looked up into the clouds as an aircraft came tearing out of the gloaming, clipping the tower of City Hall and decapitating William Penn before spiraling down into the midst of the screaming tourists swarming Benjamin Franklin Parkway, and skipping over their heads like a stone on a pond before finally plopping into the Washington Monument fountain.

◊

Ace ejected just as the plane blew up in a dazzling blast of fireworks. Landing on the art museum steps like a feather and immediately spotting the slinky Ms. Stravinsky (the only person in the vicinity not flopping around on fire like a caught fish or running and screaming that the world was over), he unpeeled his flight duds like a banana revealing his James Bondish taste in tuxedoes, hooked his arm around her waist, flashed her his point blank George Hamilton grin, and whisked her to Astral Plane on Lombard St. for dinner.

◊

"Did you happen to recognize that aircraft I crashed?" Ace asked once they'd ordered a couple of raw steaks for themselves.

"I thought it looked familiar. Tell me, what was it?"

"*The New York World's Fair 1939!* Don't you remember? It was exactly the same Lockheed L-14 Super Electra that Howard Hughes flew when he broke the world's record time and circumaviated the globe in three days, nineteen hours."

"Of course!"

"And I just totally wrecked it! Isn't that great?"

"Wow. *The New York World's Fair 1939* and the William Penn statue on Philadelphia City Hall both obliterated in one fell swoop—and I'm sure Benjamin Franklin Parkway is going to have to be repaved. Not too shabby, Ace. Do you always make a point of destroying national heritage when you fly?"

"That's why they call 'em *land*marks, baby."

Sandy grinned at him glaringly, her eyes bright and immobile even as her lips worked with reckless carnivorous abandon.

"What's wrong with wholesale destruction? That's what Sri Bhapaputrathatha always says, so that's what I say, too. Cataclysm, Ragnarok, Gotterdammerung, and Lord Shiva's Holy Apocalypse! That's the movement's mantra, Ace, and I am one of its happy children. My therapist thinks it's unhealthy, but what does he know? He can't even bite me like a man! All of creation rests on a bedrock of devastation: breakdown, death, decomposition, regeneration, and life! We have to destroy to create, Ace! We have to kill to live!"

"You're really blowing my mind tonight, Sandy. I'm surprised you're not a philosophy major."

"Oh, I was, I was, believe me. But see, that's just the problem: I blew the professors' minds clean off their little necks."

"Hm," Ace swallowed. "Interesting."

The food had arrived and, jaws full, Sandy growled contentedly.

"God, this steak is great!"

"I like a woman who eats meat."

"How can a person eat a salad? Poor defenseless plants have never had a chance against us! Animals bite! Animals kill! That's our genetic inheritance! Teeth and claws, claws and teeth! Beasts and bestiality! Plant-killing, insensitive, butchering beasts! We're all just butchering, bitching, rabid, ravenous atavistic animals! Mass destruction is one thing, Ace, but murdering innocent flora? I'd poison a man who killed a plant! It's the vegetables that ought to be eating us! Don't you think? Eh? Am I right? Well, am I right or am I right?"

"You're right. Everything about you is right tonight, Sandy."

She swooned inside and knew in her heart that Ace was her one true love and the sweetly winging unknown hope she'd secretly clasped to her breast all her miserable life, yet suddenly Sandy couldn't help asking:

"What are you looking at, my nose?"

"No, actually, I was looking at your -"

"Because we're not, you have to believe me!"

"What?"

"Jews. Never in our history have the Stravinskys ever been Jews and at no point in our future will we be, do you understand what I'm saying to you? Never ever. We're just Russians, okay?"

"Nothing wrong with that."

"You think it looks like a penis, right?"

"What does?"

"My nose! It's because of the Armenian blood. We're Russian-Armenians, okay? I don't understand what's so strange about that."

"Neither do I," Ace told her, leaning forward across his steak and placing his hand on hers.

"Just Russian and Armenian and maybe a few other things," she pouted. "Estonian. Latvian. No Jews and no gypsies, though. And I don't hate the Jews, Ace, I just want to make that piece of information as crystal clear as possible right here and right now at the beginning of the story with no confusion or quibblication of ambiguities, are you reading me?"

"Sounds like just what the doctor ordered," he cooed.

"I've never hated a single solitary Jew in my life, not once. Never ever. I just don't understand why there have to be so many, you know? Is it hatred if I happen to think we ought to be exterminated? Did I say 'we'? I mean THEM! THEM! THEM! The matzo ball eaters, you read me?"

"Oh."

"God, I hate that!" she screamed, suddenly recoiling from him, snatching up her steak knife, and plunging it into her prone left hand.

"Sandy, hate what? What's wrong?"

"You probably think I'm anti-Semitic, the way I've been carrying on tonight, don't you?"

"Not at all, Sandy," he said, watching the blood spurting playfully out of her wound. "I think you're a bright, wonderful person and that you

153

have great potential for helping humankind along the cosmic course toward peace and ultimate under-standing. Now what do you say we take that steak knife out of your hand and finish our dinner, eh?"

"Okay. But, Ace?"

"Yes?"

"I just want you to know that I'm not Jewish. Really."

"I believe you, Sandy. I think you're someone I can trust," Ace said, stroking her knee under the tablecloth, "and I'd like to make love to you tonight, as soon as possible, really slip into your personal space and feel you out and up and down and see what sort of emotional action we can get going."

"I'd give you a ride in my cockpit anytime, Ace. Anyway, I would if I could. But I'm only doing theosophical telepathic sex these days, random psychic sadomasochistic sodomy, actually, which requires an experienced medium and an orgone contracapacitor. My last therapist turned me on to it. It's highly therapeutic, you should try it sometime."

"Hm. Interesting. You mean you don't . . . ?"

"What? The old nuts-and-screws schtick? I haven't even got the equipment."

"I'm not sure I understand," he said, furtively removing his hand from her knee.

"I haven't got one, that's all," she said as her voice cracked and her smile started to fall apart.

"You mean between your . . . "

"It's sort of difficult to explain, actually. It's a long story. See, my father worked for the KGB developing high-tech espionage gadgets and electronic weapons and tracking devices that could be implanted under the agents' skins and in their heads and up their asses and, well, you know, sometimes he experimented on me at home, trying things out on me before he showed them off for the brass at work, which is totally understandable, if you stop to think about it, given the less than ideal social conditions at the time for the, the, you know, the Latvian-Estonian-Armenian-non-Jews-and-gypsies in the Soviet Union under Stalin. He couldn't afford to make any mistakes, you read me? He would have been sent to a recycling camp for sure."

"Hm," Ace cleared his throat. "And he, uh, put something, uh, in you, you say?"

"Yeah, sure, lots of things."

"Such as . . . ?"

"Well, there's a blowtorch and a pair of pliers in my left forearm and a retractable grappling hook in the right, and of course the transistor inside my skull that picks up Radio Cairo anywhere in the world. And then there are other things I haven't figured out yet, like the series of rubber tubes and clamps in my abdomen and the red Christmas light bulb at the back of my throat. He couldn't always explain these things, you understand. Tip-top secret merchandise, you read me? Not a very talkative man, my father."

"And . . . you're saying there's something, uh, attached to you," Ace asked, avoiding her eyes, "that's, uh, preventing you from . . . ?"

"It's a sort of a stainless steel stem that necks out of an iris valve mechanism and blooms into a pinwheel with blue razor-studded propeller blades."

"Hm. Well, Sandy, sorry to call foul on you," he said, getting up from the table and flinging some cash down nervously, "but that changes the ball game just a bit, doesn't it?"

"Change? Why does anything have to change between us? You meant what you said about me being a wonderful person, right? I mean, you're not just some sadistic liar who'd take a girl out only to get her into bed with you, are you? Ace, I'm still that wonderful person on the inside, I promise!"

"I'm sure you are, but – say! that reminds me," he exclaimed, suddenly checking his watch as he backed off, "I promised to have the Super Electra back at the hangar by 8.00 and I haven't got much time."

"But it exploded into little shrapnel rainbow bits, remember?"

"Well, I've gotta let the dog out! Sorry!"

He'd leapt through the door and was hailing a cab when Sandy tore out of the restaurant, dodging cars and screaming after him:

"Sri Bhapaputrathatha told me there would be moments like this! But hear me, sister bastard darkling stars of the dusky firmament! I am one of his happy children and my course is clear now!"

"My Love is Vengeance and Vengeance is God!"

Ace's cab was roaring away, but Sandy wasn't about to let this one escape, so she lobbed her grabbling hook at the bumper and skidded along the pavement after him, still howling into the blasts of exhaust.

The cabbie was swerving recklessly now, desperate to shake the harpy off, but still Sandy clung on for life or for death and stormed to the last into the breach of doom.

"Cataclysm, Ragnarok, Gotterdammerung, and Lord Shiva's Holy Apocalypse!"

CRASH!

FUTURESHOCK

TOM SANCHEZ PRUNIER

today collapses faster than calendar pages burn, annoying like my leather pants scrunching around my squeaking iron knee brace

as I throttle up my rocket-propelled V-8 Interceptor, controls wet-wired to my brain, I wend and weave my way through chrome pipe jubilee

of the fortieth generation of 30-year-olds being incinerated to maintain acceptable levels of society.

some say this is 1984, but it's really just another yesterday smoldering in the mirror. we as a species speed towards our event horizons

and we're all not walking postapocolyptically enough. others insist there's another bubble in the quantum foam dripping from a subway car

POLLUTO.

that *bouoog-oooges* and *douooog-oooges* on the laser-guided Q line
out to Coney Island, high above the snowy ruins.

truth is that the last great warrior tribe was felled by its own pride, supercolliding with the
reality that all things are not infinitesimal;

just like the known universes which, when stacked one on top of the other,
amount to just a speck on a contact lens on God's pinky,

which snaps me back into this moment [or some simulacrum thereof], pressed deep into the
bucket seat of my V-8 interceptor,

rocketing down a desolate highway towards the inevitable climax of my impossible mission
to rescue the princess' hot friend

[you know: fiendishly cute, makes all the snarky remarks?] from some dude who thinks he's
the Humungous which is fine . . .

. . . so long as he knows I think I'm Max Rockatansky and Ernest Hemingway and Lieutenant
Frank Bullitt and The Sundance Kid,

itchy trigger finger desperate to know one thing: *What time is it?*
because if this is this future, my chronometer needs a winding;

and if this is the past, I need to pull over, adjust my flux capacitor,
go back to the future and beat someone down with my tachyon skateboard.

I need to know what time it is so I can warp the edges of this universe into interlocking
quantum legos and jump from speck to speck,

eventually reaching the other, undiscovered contact lens—the one already in
God's eye, and see how I can render yesterday and tomorrow irrelevant.

POLLUTO.

maybe it's all lost in my mindprison, a meter-thick concrete wall between me and the joy of today. no matter—it's probably just another yesterday-to-be,

and I'm down at the corner bodega, knee barely a twinge, leather pants a curiosity behind the counter next to the sawed-off shotgun;

these too-cool relics at rest, desperate for the untimely motion
of tomorrow's cataclysm.

THE END

THE COPPER HEART

DREW RHYS WHITE

On a night when the city was flogged by rain, when spring dawned like an invader, when all of Philadelphia cowered before the onslaught of March, Lester Clay was seized by agents of the Bureau of Affectional Rectitude and taken into custody. Lester knew better than to be out after curfew, knew better than to be fishing for cod—as he called it—given the recent spate of ordinances against public lewdness and homosexualist conduct of all flavors. But he had emerged onto Richmond Street after a double shift at the iron works cold, sweat-sodden, and spent, to behold a red-haired beauty bright as a hurricane lamp in the storm, just standing on Richmond. Lester knew that if he went back to the boardinghouse he would be out in the downpour looking for the boy before twenty minutes had passed. The youth loitered in the rufescent glow of an apothecary's doorway, and the moment Lester took a step toward him, lit off into undulating curtains of rain. Wasn't it always the red-haired ones who could stir, not only Lester's sex, but the sclerotic heart within him? And this one had something no other had—a warm, mesmeric glow, as if the boy's thick chest hid some cunningly wrought secret, investing him with an occult incandescence.

POLLUTO.

Lester followed the lad through the warehouse district and toward the river —where the waves of the Delaware rose up to smack the sky and the lad's red locks whipped round his head like flame on a match. When his quarry, with an inviting glance over his shoulder, entered the dead forest of pilings along the tidal sand, Lester felt sure that there the boy would yield every burning fissure of his body to him.

But Lester was the quarry; Lester the pursued. Agents of the Bureau stepped round the pilings, slapping black clubs into their palms. Still, Lester kept his eye on the boy—who disappeared in darkness without a look back as Lester's chin hit the sand.

◊

He was a powerful, unlovely man, his body formed by hard work, hunger, and disease. Rickets had bowed his legs. Toil at the Quaker City Iron Works had broadened his shoulders to a degree more brutish than manly. And a congenital mineral deficiency had prematurely wrinkled his hide—compromising its natural elasticity so that at 36 his jaw hung slack as clothesline and the skin drooped from his eye sockets.

But for all that nature had cursed Lester with asymmetry and premature rugosity, she had blessed him with two exceptional gifts. The first was his unusual strength, which made him a hero to the increasingly persecuted homosexualist mino-rity throughout the city, and the champion of the Uranian League in their skirmishes with the police. The second was a singular and celebrated skill that perhaps brought him more recognition than the first, and, ironically, was born of his inability to assimilate certain minerals. The same con-genital defect that had defaced his skin also lent a fantastic suppleness to his frame. This freed him to perform a much-envied feat of sexual solipsism—one he exhibited weekly at the "Bear Cave," an establishment on 12th street which catered to men of all classes whose sole common characteristics were their interest in each other, and the outlaw status this now conferred on them.

Lester's powerful body and impuls-ive nature conspired to make him insensible to danger, with the result that although the Uranian League—once

161

powerful in city politics—was proscribed, and its members criminalized, he did not change his habits—but frequented the same taprooms, brothels, and groves of public concupiscence as he had when homosexualists dominated City Hall. It had been difficult for Lester to grasp that the glory days—when Uranian-trained and led regiments had acquitted themselves with such gallantry in Hawaii and Manila, when, indeed, homosexualists had been celebrated as the finest sons of the Republic and godfathers of the Empire—were over.

The gay Nineties had met their end.

And so, it was in the basement of the newly-formed Bureau of Affectional Rectitude that Lester Clay first saw moving pictures. The opening reel showed two men—who re-sembled a pair of tool-and-die makers Lester knew from the Bear Cave—in their shirt-sleeves doing a cakewalk. But neither responded when Lester bellowed at them to clear the hell out before they got tied up too. The men turned and turned in each other's arms, though there was no music, and—Lester realized as he regained his wits more fully—*no available space where they appeared to be.* Lester began to understand that they weren't *present* in the same way as he and—this other man—whom he now noticed seated not four feet from where he was bound—when they disappeared and were replaced by a pair of naked wrestlers.

Dozing in his chair, the man from the Bureau was missing a fine show. Nothing like a couple of strapping specimens of Am-erican manhood gripping each other up and giving each other their best. Lester consid-ered letting the man rest. He looked like he needed it, what with his twitchy mouth, and overall nervous, persnickety look. But the man from the bureau was Lester's only hope of securing some information about his tenancy, and, Lester thought—realizing that he was naked—a blanket.

And, neurasthenic though he app-eared, the man had a promising meaty bulge in his trousers that Lester hoped to get better acquainted with. He had been in the clink before, and it was his policy to make the best of a bad situation.

"You there. Wake up."

The man jerked himself into con-sciousness as if by some panic-triggered reflex. "Yes, good day Sir," he said, "I was awake, Mr. Waxwroth, not meaning to contradict of course—"

He stopped, eyes popping in a moment of recognition.

"I'm not Mr. Waxwroth," said Lester.

"I know that," said the man. "I see that very clearly."

And then, to Lester's surprise and delight, he saw the man take a long look at his penis, reclining in all its furrowed glory on Lester's stomach. The man picked up a wooden clipboard and made a notation.

"See something you like?" said Lester.

"No," said the man. "I am charged with the responsibility of recording all physiological changes to your person."

"Not drawing a picture to look at later, then?"

"No."

"If you say so."

The man looked at Lester sourly, then looked away.

"Who do you answer to?"

"I am not allowed to reveal any information about your internment here."

"Is it Mr. Waxwroth?"

"You're not supposed to know about Mr. Waxwroth."

"Too late; I do. Will you get in trouble?"

The man shifted in his seat. "No," he said. "Yes."

"Then I won't tell. On one condition. Tell me your name."

"No."

"Then I'll tell Mr. Waxwroth that you've told me all about him."

"But I haven't—but I haven't told you anything—but—" Already dragged into the whirlpool of Lester's argumentation, the man seemed to search his thoughts for some root or branch with which to pull himself from the undertow— "You're the *prisoner*."

"Which makes your lack of dis-cretion that much more blameworthy."

The man slumped against the wall. "It's Silas," he said. "The name is Silas."

"Silas what?"

The man blinked at Lester, furiously.

"Why don't you get me a blanket, Silas?"

"Rules."

"Not because you like looking at a fellow in his birthday suit?"

"No! No."

"I'm cold, Silas. Look at how shriv-eled my poor pecker is. It gets bigger than that, you know."

"I wouldn't know."

"Wouldn't know about peckers? Haven't got one?"

"I do!" said Silas.

"Then let's see it."

Silas stood, stepping a few feet away. "I'm not supposed to be talking to you."

"Get me a blanket and I'll stop talking."

"Can't. Rules."

"Show me your pecker then."

"No! You have to stop talking. Watch the film."

"Don't you like showing peckers?"

"No!"

"Oh I think you do, Silas. I can always tell a man who likes peckers."

"You have to be quiet."

"I know you like peckers because you have the sign."

"There's no sign." But Silas's eyes narrowed in what may have been fear or suspicion, it didn't matter which as Lester had the same feeling a rock climber gets when he knows his fingers have found the hold that will enable him to scramble further up the cliff.

"It's because your left nut hangs lower than your right."

"It's not true—" Silas goggled in horror and clutched himself. "Oh God— does it show? That's the sign?"

"I was a tailor's assistant," Lester laughed, "before I got too big and ugly. Most men dangle lower on the left than the right. But I think we've learned something here, Silas."

Silas returned to his stool in defeat.

"I feel we're going to be great friends."

Lester's laughter was interrupted by the sound of a door clanging open. Footsteps echoed through the basement; a woman in a white coat paused by Lester's feet. She was trim and handsome, with hard lines around her eyes and mouth.

"Awake, is he?" she said.

"Yes'm," murmured Silas—almost too quietly to be heard.

"Any changes?"

"No ma'am."

"Continue as instructed. Mr. Waxwroth will be by."

"Yes'm."

The woman's footsteps trailed away, punctuated by the clang of the door.

Lester watched Silas narrowly. "Who was that?"

"Someone you're not to know about," Silas said.

"I will though—I'm good at know-ing things, wouldn't you say?"

Silas jumped from his chair and threw his clipboard down; it struck the cement floor with a bang. "You can't *talk* to me like that

—I have power—!" He thrust his face toward Lester's and said, in a hushed tone perhaps intended for menace: "I have power over you and I can do things!"

"Well Mr. Dangly-Nut," Lester responded, in an equally hushed tone, but conveying intimacy: "It looks as though we both can do things. I can say I know you."

"It's not true."

"Your guilty terror will make it seem true. I could say I've seen you at some of the places I go."

"You haven't—you couldn't have—you couldn't have seen me."

Another fingerhold. "Been out on the town, then?"

"No!" Silas was screaming now, bearing his teeth with a look of nauseated terror.

"All right," said Lester. "I'm not going to do you any harm. Just loosen these straps and I'll be out of your hair."

Silas fell back into his chair, holding his stomach.

"Or, you could just give my pecker a bit of the old hand shake—ease me into this life of confinement."

Silas's head was between his legs now.

"You're going to have to do *something* for me, friend, seeing as we know each other so well and we're practically old acquaintances."

"I can't. I can't," Silas said, his voice muffled by the seat of his chair.

"Just get me a blanket. And then we're done talking for now."

Silas obeyed him, rising, and returning with a gray felt blanket, which he threw over Lester's massive form as if it were a white flag of surrender. He then crumpled into his chair, and was absorbed into the universal sleep of the exhausted.

Lester, pleased with this small victory—which he hoped to parlay into ever greater victories till he landed back on Richmond Street—became absorbed into the film being projected on the slick wall of the basement.

One of the wrestlers was older and beefier, and getting the better of his opponent—a wiry towhead who reminded Lester of a German he'd bent over a tombstone in Laurel Hill Cemetery. The memory had a leavening effect on Lester's penis; he began to wonder if, given the leverage he had over him, he could persuade Silas to lend him a hand—or better.

"Halloo, Boy Blue, wake up, come blow your horn."

Trembling into wakefulness with a start, the bespectacled lackey of the Bureau of Affectional Rectitude glanced down at Lester's erection with alarm, and turned a crank by the lathe. The lathe tilted, Lester's feet swung up, and Lester felt something cold at the back of his head. Water—which soon blurred his sight, filled his nostrils, and muffled his outraged protestations.

"Do you know why you're here, Mr. Clay?" asked the voice.

Lester tried to muster an answer. He couldn't. He tried to locate the voice in the room.

"You have the build of a sports-man."

Lester found the speaker, sitting by his side in a brown pinstriped suit that flattered his well-knit frame, red hair aglow in the gloom. It was the cruel boy from the other night—and if he was older than he had seemed, he was just as compelling a presence.

Not a beautiful boy, a beautiful man. Lester's captor.

"I'm Mr. Waxwroth," the beautiful man said.

But Lester would have known this without being told. Waxwroth smelled of bergamot, cloves, and concentrated power.

"Do you enjoy athletics?"

The terror of his recent baptism, and the sting it had left in his throat made response impossible.

"I should apologize for our ruse of the other evening, Mr. Clay," said Waxwroth, settling back into his chair. "But as you are clearly a man of sport—with that muscul-ature—you should understand that one must sacrifice for the good of the team. To impersonate a street boy —to deceive—you can imagine how distasteful that was for me, a man of probity, a family man.

"Or, perhaps you can't imagine that. . .

"At any rate, your penchant for males of my complexion was known to us through our research. All part of the game—life is sport, no? You gain, I lose, and vice versa . . . "

Waxwroth nodded, and Silas came from a corner of the room to turn the crank by the lathe, bringing Lester into an upright position.

"We play 'for keeps,' as they say, Clay. My loyalty to my team—country, comrades, *family*—trumps all other con-siderations."

"Let me go."

"We will." Waxwroth directed Silas to position two sawhorses in front of Lester, and to lay a board across them. Silas obeyed, then left the room.

"Before you go, we will invite you officially to join *our* team. We could use a man with a wide range of contacts. But we want you to be one of us. When you've suc-cessfully completed your treatment, we'll extend an invitation."

"What if I don't, join?"

"Then we'll continue your treat-ment till you do—or till you pose no threat to us."

Silas returned with a tray and set it on the table. He thrust a spoon into a bowl, and held the spoon before Lester. A flour-thickened corn chowder congealed on the spoon as Lester looked at it. One yellow kernel, failing to cling to the metal lip, dropped onto Lester's chest and was lost in a trough.

"Wait," said Waxwroth. He leaned over Lester and fixed him with a pair of mellow gray eyes. Lester imagined he heard a whirring and a ticking, as if Waxwroth had a particularly noisome pocket watch in his waistcoat. But—the sound came from deep inside the man's skin.

"Clay, before we dine, won't you tell us a little about the activities of the club you frequent, this 'Bear Cave.'"

◊

Lester answered Waxwroth with half-truths and plausible lies. Waxwroth failed to see through Lester, or was willing to bide his time—Lester couldn't be sure. The only homosexualists whose names Lester surrendered were known police informants. This Lester did with a great show of dread and shame. Waxwroth continued to visit at mealtimes, asking sometimes repeated, and other times new questions. The pattern of the interrogations was always the same. Waxwroth would begin with general questions about homosexualist activity around the city, and then circle in on the Uranian League. Lester began to suspect that the main thrust of the inquiries, though cloaked by other topics, was to learn the specifics of the Uranian plan to provoke some foreign entity to an affront to nationalist spirit, which would embroil the nation in further war, in which Uranian mercenary contractors could once again prove their prowess in both strategy and tactics.

Fortunately, Lester knew almost nothing of the Uranian stratagem to regain power beyond that simple outline, and felt secure in his relative ignorance—secure from committing any significant betrayal regardless of the techniques his adversaries might apply.

Lester's days at the Bureau blended together like the still frames of a moving picture. In the early part of the day he would be treated to homoerotic films and punished with the water torture if he responded with any outward show of arousal. In the evenings Silas would feed him his daily meal, during which heteroerotic films would be presented. These latter he found mildly interesting at points, at other points, nauseating.

Having successfully secured a blanket from Silas at his first interrogation, Lester continued his program of bending the bureau minion to his will, in hopes of gaining his freedom, or at least, sex.

He achieved this secondary goal late one night after the bureau added a second round of homoerotic aversion treat-ment to Lester's daily regimen. Neither Wax-wroth nor the woman with the hard face appeared at these sessions, lending Silas, Lester speculated—in wonder at what came to pass—a sense of greater liberty and daring.

Lester was startled, more than startled—though he had been entreating it over some weeks—when, instead of turning the crank by the lathe and subjecting Lester to a dunking, Silas responded to Lester's erection by locking the doors, greasing Lester with a leftover smudge of gravy from the dinner tray, then stepping from his trousers and hopping onto the lathe while gingerly drawing apart his buttocks.

Lester was equally startled—and impressed—when instead of inching himself onto Lester's obelisk with mincing reticence, Silas, in one motion, subsumed him utterly.

"Silas—my boy," Lester gasped—"I didn't know you had it in you."

"I have it now," said Silas, glasses fogging, and smiling a little at his witticism.

Bound to a board, there was little Lester could do to assist their labor, but Silas evidently contained a mad sprung energy that made him more than equal to the effort.

They finished, after several minutes of frantic pistoning, with Lester's three-week reserve spent inside Silas, and whatever Silas had salted away now lost on the corrugated wasteland of Lester's torso.

The bureau man slid off Lester without a word, and hoisted himself into his pants.

He then sat on the stool by the lathe, and, if it had not been for his shirtfront heaving like a bellows, one might not have known that anything had happened to him at all.

"There's only one thing left I can ask of you," said Lester, when he had recovered enough to speak.

"I know," said Silas.

"Well?"

"It's the one thing I can't give."

"Wouldn't it be better if I were out of here, knowing what I know of you?"

"You won't tell them anything."

Lester was silent.

"Would you?"

"I don't know that I would. I guess I couldn't. I don't like your bosses, but I've become fond of you."

"I'm fond of you too."

"As you have intimated, by subtle signs."

Silas leaned against the wall. "They helped me. They helped my family. I was like you—a perverted invert—or—inverted per-vert—? They gave me the water treatment and that fixed me."

"Temporarily?"

"I don't go to the docks. I have hobbies—I fix motors and take apart gadgets —collect machines. Tinker with things."

"What things?"

"Toys that walk about, or move on wheels, do tricks. A steam-heated slate with a spring, to toast your bread. A clock with a calliope that plays *The Union Forever* to wake you in the morning. Small, useful things."

170

"Like you."

Silas blushed. "They're what I have—to make up for things other people have that I don't."

"You have me now."

"I can't change anything about my life. My father and my old uncles—they know where all of us live. I can't cross the Bureau."

"You're frightened of Waxwroth."

"He's always been kind to me, but I've seen him deal with men in your situation. He can be rough."

"Loosen my bonds and I could take care of him."

"I don't doubt it. But there's an army of Waxwroths. Knock him down and two more take his place. Even when we were powerful there were always more of *them*. They don't need us now, that's what they think. All the wars are over, it's a new century, and they can tug their oceans around them and raise their families."

At this, Lester's Uranian inculcation flooded to the forefront of his mind. "That's why we need some threat that only we can save them from. Make them rely on us again. Then when we're back on top, that Wax-wroth'll be the first one we take down."

"It wouldn't take much—he's not as sturdy as he looks."

"How so?"

"Heart troubles. People say he used to have fainting spells. They put a motor inside him to put him to rights."

"They can do that?"

"Tinkering with hearts is what they do."

"What's it look like—?"

"Copper, with gears and all kinds of moving parts as I understand it."

They fell silent—Silas almost nod-ding off, Lester picturing the queer object whose presence he had intuited within Wax-wroth from the first, as if the thing had summoned him here. He pictured himself and Silas in Silas's home, looking at Silas's gadgets and devices, the copper heart displayed proudly among them, keeping time like a metronome.

Silas snored; Lester felt a surge of panic at the thought of being left without his friend's consciousness by him.

"Free me."

"They'll kill me."

"Come with me."

"I daren't."

"Then don't free me. Loosen me. I can wriggle out—I'm a bit more flexible than they're counting on."

"I know—" Silas hesitated. "I saw your show."

"At the Bear Cave?"

"It was very, memorable."

"You should have stuck around."

"I shouldn't have been there at all."

"Did you leave anything in my hat?"

"No. I kept well in the back."

"Then you owe me."

"You've already got all that's coming to you tonight."

◊

In the morning they were awake-ned by a banging on the door of the basement cell. The door sailed open, and an angry Waxwroth strode into the room.

"Where was your report?" he demanded of Silas. "Why wasn't it on my desk this morning?"

Silas looked around helplessly for his clipboard.

Waxwroth looked from Silas to the dinner tray—still on the sawhorse table from the night before. "Have you been in here *all night?*"

Silas's mute terror provoked Wax-wroth to fury. His eyebrows sparked in the morning light from the basement windows, his alabaster forehead reddened. He looked at Lester; Lester, normally innocent of the least taint of modesty, felt at once self-conscious of the oleaginous sheen on his flaccid penis.

"You're *still* one of them, you pipsqueak," Waxwroth shrilled, backhanding his underling with full force.

At this, Lester roared, roared to see Silas mistreated, Silas who was now crum-pled against the wet wall like a discarded suit of clothes. "Get up!" Waxwroth screamed, at a womanly pitch, "Up!"

Silas unfolded from the floor, and stood, shaking before Waxwroth. "Help me move him," Waxwroth said.

"I can't—I can't lift him."

Waxwroth pulled his arm back again in warning, prompting further roars and threats from Lester. But a cowed Silas obeyed, moving to Lester's feet as Waxwroth went to his head.

"Now," said Waxwroth.

They lifted and carried the lathe, with Lester, then dragged it—as Silas fumbled his end—to the center of the room. Waxwroth kicked Lester onto his face, and Lester heard the sound of a rope yanked through a pulley. A coldness was slipped into the ropes that tied Lester's hands. Then, with horrific pain, his arms were torn into the air, his body torn after them. Lester swung from the ceiling, and came face to face with Waxwroth.

Waxwroth's face had become a plate of egg-whites, its features random obj-ects melting into the blankness. "We will make you our own, or we will end you," the face said. "Your outrage at my handling of your *pathic* here betrays the intensity of your attachment to him."

Waxwroth shoved Lester; with each swing of the rope Lester's bonds cut into his flesh; he felt a wrenching ache at his shoulders. "When we release the purified Lester Clay into the world once again, *he* will remain. *He* will be the motor that drives you."

Lester, half-blind from pain, sensed as a radiating warmth the copper heart in Waxwroth's chest.

"A living piece of you will reside within these walls, without your ever being able to reach it."

It wasn't what Waxwroth said, so much as the quietly hypnotic tone he used—shimmering though the blinding pain Lester felt—that caused Lester's senses to brighten, within their synesthesic mist, to a con-centrated intensity. It was as if, within the ever-flowering, multiform haloes of color, sound, and heat that emanated from Wax-wroth, a cyclonic tunnel, an omphalos of insight opened. In his state of agonized derangement, Lester saw the copper device within Waxwroth as the source of all this coruscating heat and power, an unearthly talisman that, if seized, would cause the walls of his prison to blow apart, the outside world to flood in, and he and Silas to be united not as two joined together, but as one indis-soluble being formed of light and aery force.

He heard the slap of his foot-bindings hit the floor—the sound registering as an echo of green and black circles in his sight. Silas had loosed his bonds after all —but when—while he slept. Silas was with him. He hoisted his legs into the air and struck Waxwroth's chest with the flats of his feet.

The thrust of the blow enabled him to turn his wrists so that first one, then the other slipped through their fetter. Lester fell to the floor, his legs buckling beneath him.

Naked, wet, and lined as an engraving, Lester dragged himself to the spot on the basement floor where a winded Waxwroth lay clutching his chest. Seeing his enemy approach, Waxwroth raised himself on one arm, only to fall again as Lester dropped on his legs with the full weight of his body.

Waxwroth, on his back, opened his mouth, though whether in shock or in readiness to call for help Lester couldn't guess. Waxwroth fumbled at his side; Lester crawled up him to seize whatever weapon Waxwroth was groping for before his adversary could. Too late. The red-haired man brandished a small, pearl-handled pistol. Lester grasped his arm, but not in time to prevent the gun from firing. The sounds became white hot starbursts in Lester's eyes. He looked at Silas, realizing that the little man would likely be the last pleasing thing he would see before he died. His beloved's hair and mousy moustache glowed gold against the green basement wall.

The gun continued to sound. Lester took Waxwroth's wrist and bent it behind his back, turning the man face down on the cement. Waxwroth's heartbeats clanged like brass in Lester's ear, the heart itself seemed to burn through Waxwroth's shirt and jacket like a fiery flower. Lester grasped the waist of

Waxwroth's pants with his free hand; Wax-wroth screamed; Lester yanked his trousers so that his suspenders snapped like whips, and buttons flew like bullets. Punching through Waxwroth's roseate ferrule, he thrust his arm into the shrieking man, grasping, rummaging, searching for the shining mechanical treasure within the bowels of the white casket.

Now he was on his feet, warm blood running down his naked forearms, an orange blossom cradled in his monstrous hands. He held the crepitating bloom to Silas; who looked beyond him in alarm. The woman from the bureau stepped between them and knocked the object from Lester's grasp.

"Guards," she yelled over her shoulder. "Boys," she said to Lester and Silas, "your silent friends are everywhere; more numerous than your enemies dream." She dragged the sawhorses to the window, stood on one, and slammed the second through the glass without losing her composure. "How can you godfather an Empire, without first there being a midwife?"

The woman ran to the door and called for the guards again. Lester tossed Silas over the shards, then heaved his bloodied bulk through the broken window.

THE END

VASTY DEEP

REN HOLTON

Heidi Naismith waited to see if the young man would take advantage of the darkness to hold her hand. Of the four men she'd met since arriving at the Society for the Support of Young Ladies, he was definitely the best. He had a profession, unlike the poultry-keeper, the vat cleaner and the young man who worked for his father in an indefinable capacity because nobody else would employ him. He had a reasonable degree of intelligence, and, best of all, his work, as an engineer on the automated steam railway in Bengal, meant he was away from England for months on end. His wife wouldn't have him always underfoot.

Heidi was realistic about her chances of success. If she didn't find a man to marry her before she turned twenty-one, the inevitable slide down the social ladder would have reached unstoppable speed. She'd been accused of waywardness after her mother's death, for insisting that it has been pneumonia brought out by bad housing, not 'lingering consumption as a result of abandonment as a young wife' that had killed the woman. And yet, instead of the debtor's prison or insane asylum that she'd expected to find herself in after her protest, she was here, beside a youth with prospects, about to watch an aquarium show.

If he thought she would make a good wife, she would be safe. Well, relatively so. Marriage hadn't been a haven for her mother, but all Heidi needed to do was marry respectably and guard her tongue. And marriage was preferable to the alternative—life unchaperoned on London's streets where touts offered 'guaranteed virgins' for sale, rogue automata passed as human, and a slaver could lean from his steam car and have a girl plucked from the streets for his opium den, while the Peelers watched from their blue-painted police boxes.

As the aquarium became fully dark, Heidi let her elbow bump into her escort. Almost reflexively he took her arm and she smiled into the velvet blackness. An automaton began to speak, its rich tones sounding oddly muffled until she remembered it was inside the water tank, amongst the invisible fish. But the fish were no longer invisible— tiny points of light, like distant candles, began to appear in the tank, pink and blue and white. People pressed closer to the glass to observe, as the man-shaped machine walked around inside, describing shrimp and jellyfish and the marvels of the immense water pressure inside the huge glass vessel which kept the deep-sea creatures alive.

Heidi noticed something else. Something she'd seen a dozen times, every night of her life, since she'd come to SSYL. It was the silhouette of a woman, arms raised as if closing curtains to shut out the dark. It was what she saw from her bedroom window, gazing out across the inner quadrangle every evening as the Society's deserving maidens prepared for bed. But this woman was in the tank.

"There's a woman in there," she said.

The young man beside her chuckled. "You're seeing things, my dear." Now he did take her hand, and pat it. "The little lights are fooling your eyes."

Heidi looked again. The was no doubt. The black shape of a crinolined woman with upraised arms floated against the starry luminescence of the underwater world.

"There's a dead woman in the tank," she said firmly.

There were gasps and mutters from their invisible neighbours. The automaton faltered in its presentation. A woman screamed.

Then there was pandemonium. An epidemic of female shrieking broke

177

out, accompanied by the sound of over-corseted ladies fainting and men cursing. People rushed for the exits, trampling unconscious women underfoot. There was a strange, flat, cracking sound as the automaton pounded on the nearest glass wall, smashing its way out, its head twisted unnaturally to peer back over its shoulder at the dark figure in the dark water.

◈

"The gentlemen are still being interviewed by the police," said Lady Arbuthnot, founder of SSYL, as she sat in her steam carriage, smiling vaguely out of the window. Heidi wondered if the smile was a social artifice or a sign of impending senility. Still it had been very good of the woman to come and collect her. "You must have excellent eyesight," Lady A said.

"I beg your pardon?" Heidi watched the smile, it didn't change but cold grey eyes were assessing her and, she felt, concluding she wasn't up to the mark.

She straightened her back and met the older woman's gaze. "I do. But that is not the whole matter. I am also intelligent and observant."

"Indeed?" Lady A smiled even more benignly. "And what did you observe?"

"Several things. First, that we, the audience, were not supposed to be there—it was only because the weather was too inclement for the firework display we were supposed to be attending and some Yahoo prevailed on the automaton to open the display for us. Second, the woman in the tank was poor, which is odd, given the opulence of the exhibit . . . "

"Third . . . ?" queried Lady A.

"I'll keep the third observation to myself for now," Heidi said.

There was a brief silent battle of wills which ended in a tacit draw.

"Your first observation is interesting," Lady A said. "*The Wonders of the Vasty Deep* is an educational exhibition. I was a little surprised to discover such an important establishment was entirely under the charge of an automaton; that does not speak well of the Directors of the enterprise. I shall be asking questions about it. Your second observation in eludes me."

"Well, she was a woman respectable enough to wear a crinoline and heavy skirts, their outline was

178

unmistakable in the water, but her arms had floated upwards, as had her hair, which was unpinned and short." Heidi felt herself shiver and for the first time the horror of her grotesque discovery struck her. Until now she'd been dispassionate but the woman in the tank suddenly became real, and dead, in memory, in a way she hadn't truly been during the discovery. It was the awful contrast between the beauty of the marine creatures and the black vacancy of the woman's shape that affected her now.

"So you think she'd sold her hair for wig-making," Lady A said.

"Yes. Or maybe she had some work where long hair wasn't allowed. Don't the new miniature-clockwork factories insist on women covering their hair and men being clean-shaven?"

Lady A nodded, "A good point. But either way, we can safely say no woman would cut her crowing glory unless it was economically necessary."

Heidi's hand rose to her own hair. Would she one day be reduced to selling it by the inch to some hairdresser? "The young man who escorted me, Mr Prendergast?" she asked.

"Still at the police station, as I said. Very impressed by your powers of observation. But . . . " Lady A leaned forward and stopped smiling. "Not so impressed by your willingness to argue with him."

"He was wrong," Heidi said, staring out of the smoked-glass window to hide her tears.

"He *was* wrong," said Lady A. "And he was wrong *for* you and wrong *about* you. I shall speak to the people at the Society for the Settlement of Young Men with Prospects, and tell them that you deserve much better than that fool."

"Please," Heidi shook her head. "If you upset them, they might not produce any more young men who need a wife."

"My dear girl, they will do whatever I tell them to, because SSYMP only exists to meet the needs of SSYL. And if I had my way, no young lady would ever need marriage to support her—perhaps one day we'll change this fossilised society enough to allow females to stand alone, socially, economically and emotionally."

Heidi skinned her teeth in her own social smile. "Thank you, Lady Arbuthnot, but my expectations are more realistic. I am the daughter of a

179

father who abandoned his family and a Fenian mother. I have been censured by the beadle of my parish for a wayward tongue and I have no dowry or means of support. In six months I shall be twenty-one and SSYL will not longer be able to offer me a home. If I am not married, or at least engaged, by then . . ." She stared the older woman down, both of them knowing that her chances of a good life were limited indeed.

They passed the rest of the journey in silence.

◊

The next morning the story was in the newspapers, and even received a mention on the eight o'clock radio broadcast, fed into the SSYL dining room by means of a huge steam-powered amplifier run from a boiler that the residents took it in turns to stoke. The radio announcer said the woman had been identified and enquiries would continue, but that foul play was not suspected.

"That means enquiries will not continue," Heidi muttered to herself. "Just another woman taking her own life and who cares about that?"

She cared, and very badly. She had expected the other SSYL girls to question her, but nobody did—they were all too busy worrying over their own futures to care about the past of an anonymous female. The image of the woman haunted her through the morning as she worked on the various duties assigned to her by the charity. The only interrogation came at luncheon, when she was asked to describe Mr Prendergast in case he requested to meet another SSYL lodger before his leave was up.

"Don't argue with him," she finished up, after an incisive verbal portrait. The other girls nodded. None of them asked about the dead woman.

At tea-time, Lady A's chauffeur was waiting in the hall. He beckoned Heidi out of the throng and led her to the steam carriage where Lady A waited.

"Your mother was a Fenian," she said, as they drove off. "How unorthodox."

Heidi settled her skirts and refused to speak.

"A Fenian and an ardent suffragist—a fascinating combination." Lady A suggested.

"My mother was very young when she married," Heidi said, finally. "She learned to be more circumspect as she got older." And she had learnt, fast. Three months married, less than eighteen years old, newly arrived in London from Ireland, Roisin Naismith had discovered that while the Irish might be disliked, actual Fenians were detested. She'd stopped talking about Irish independence, but it was too late, her neighbours whispered behind her back and when her surveyor husband returned from working in Dorset, told him to move his wife out of the district. James Naismith assessed the situation and decided persecution would follow his red-haired, heavily-accented bride wherever she went. He moved without her and without leaving a forwarding address. Heidi would rather have had her teeth pulled out with pliers than say this to a third party—her mother had drummed into her that keeping quiet was a survival trait and she'd learnt the lesson well.

"Where are we going?" she asked.

"The police have ceased questioning any of the gentlemen and do not intend to talk to any of the ladies." Lady A's tone was ironic. "They will not visit the place where the poor young victim was found either."

Heidi sniffed and Lady A nodded as though she had said something of great value, before continuing to enunciate with the clarity of disgust. "I sent a telegram asking why no female witnesses would be interviewed. The Chief Constable himself replied that such a shock to the sensibilities must surely have rendered any lady incapable of accurate observation, while women of the lower orders, who are more used to violent death, are simply not reliable—they sensationalise their emotions instead of reporting the facts."

Heidi nodded; it was the standard male judgement on the fairer sex.

"Which is why," Lady A continued, "you and I shall undertake our own investigation."

Heidi scowled out of the window. Lady A's quixotic scheme would cost her important husband-hunting time, but she could hardly say no to the founder of the organisation that had offered her succour.

"And you shall be paid, as my investigative amanuensis, at the rate of a sovereign a week, or part thereof."

Heidi calculated quickly. A sovereign would pay a quarter's rent on a room in a decent house in Lambeth or Balham. At that level of pay she need not fear the future nearly so much.

The carriage passed another, open-topped, in which sat an automaton carrying a huge leather tube with brass bindings—dress designs or architects' plans or sheet music for a symphony orchestra, Heidi guessed.

"You don't like automata, do you?" Asked Lady A.

"Not much."

"Why not?"

Heidi paused; she'd never tried to express her visceral repugnance rationally. "Because they sometimes act like people, like that one there—sitting in his carriage like a Lord, and sometimes like machines. It's dissimulation, pretending, lying."

"And the one at Vasty Deep, did that react like a human or a machine?" Lady A said.

Heidi paused again. The other woman was astute—the automaton hadn't behaved as it should, and its behaviour had led her to her third troubling observation.

"Not like a person," she said slowly. "Because it was walking around in the water, pointing to sea creatures that glowed in the dark—no human could possibly do that! And yet . . . "

"It behaved out of character?" suggested Lady A.

"Yes. Yes it did! When I said about the body in the tank, it panicked. It beat its fists against the glass until it broke and the water poured out. Surely a machine wouldn't have been frightened of a dead woman?"

"No, that is very unlikely. What does a machine fear most?"

Heidi knew the answer immediately. "Breaking down, damage, not working properly—anything that could lead to it being turned back into parts." Not much different, really, to the fears of the poor.

"But it was adapted to water and a corpse couldn't harm it, so why was it terrified into breaking the tank?"

Heidi began to say, "There's something else . . . " but the carriage pulled up outside the exhibition hall. It looked quite different without the drama of twilight and the imminent storm. Heidi stepped from the carriage and stared at the building. Lady A dismounted more slowly and stood aside, tapping her fan on the side of the vehicle.

"What are you thinking, young lady?" she asked as Heidi bent to examine the opening hours.

"It's almost as if the owners don't want people to visit. The sign-

182

writing is illegible and even though I'm not tall, I have to stoop to read it."

Lady A snapped the fan open. "The Vasty Deep is a requirement of the monopoly given to the Marine Exploration Consortium, a company granted an Imperial charter to investigate, fish, assay and mine the Ryukyu ocean trench between her Majesty's dominion of Taiwan and the Protectorate of Japan. In return for the sale of shares and debentures, the board of Trustees is required to mount a permanent display to educate the populace about the value, utility and mystery of the deep oceans."

Heidi sniffed and pushed the door. It was locked. She raised her eyebrows at Lady A and headed down a nearby alley. After a few seconds she heard the old woman follow.

As she'd expected, there was a shuttered delivery entrance at the rear of the building and, beside it, a mean entrance, as squalid as a pawnbroker's chalk-board. Heidi leaned against it and forced it open. She reached into her reticule to find the candle and matches she'd taken from the SSYL pantry, but before she could use the latter to light the former, a white beam lanced through the darkness, skewering the dirty wall in its merciless glare.

"Halogen torch," said Lady A, lifting the light so it shone directly in Heidi's eyes. "The very latest development."

Heidi shielded her face with both hands. "Very good, but could you not point it at me?"

"I do beg your pardon," Lady A held the torch lower. "I'm not really used to such devices."

Heidi swore under her breath and picked her way forward, fighting purple and blue afterimages, along a corridor that smelt of mice droppings and mouldering shoes. The rattan runner squelched underfoot. She bent and touched it—there was a mossy, slimy texture to it that made her shudder. The torchlight descended, illuminating the silvery sheen of water.

"Capillary action," said Lady A.

Heidi wished she had a fan to snap closed, but had to content herself with an unseen scowl.

"You're an unusual young woman," Lady A continued.

Heidi stopped. What was she supposed to reply? It was one of the moments her mother had warned her of, 'Speak out, my darling, and they'll likely crucify you for your unladylike ways, but stay quiet and they'll walk all over you, ignoring your dignity, your desires and your very humanity.' It was a gamble, everything was a gamble, in a game her mother had played and lost. So Heidi prevaricated. "I don't know what you mean."

"You're single-minded and you'd like to think of yourself as cold-blooded, but the death of a stranger troubles you enough to distract you from your aims. You ask few questions and answer even fewer and yet you're clearly quick-witted and possessed of considerable resources of intellect. I wonder what makes you so . . . unwilling to engage in comradeship."

She picked her way past Heidi, their skirts touching, the cyan coloured beam dancing like lightning along the sordid corridor. Heidi felt the slow burn of indignation raising from her belly, past her ribs, to surge like a volcano into her throat. She opened her mouth to reply and immediately threw her hand over her eyes as Lady A played the stark light over her face. The older woman spoke.

"Yes dear?"

"Your interest is most gratifying," Heidi said, forcing her anger back down to where it could do her no harm.

"And your reticence is highly provoking, but no matter, we shall understand each other better before this is over."

Heidi found a smile and didn't allow it to fade until the torchlight moved from her face. "Perhaps I should take the torch," she suggested. "Your lovely moiré silk will be quite ruined by this damp if you don't lift it from the floor."

Lady A's expression was unreadable in the gloom, but her tone was sardonic. "Of course dear, please do lead the way."

Heidi moved to the front, aware that Lady A seemed more interested in baiting her than in the supposed investigation. She'd heard about such women, men too, who—old and weary of respectability—lived lives of vicarious wickedness through young protégées whom they incited to gambling, intoxication or sexual profligacy. What better place to test the morals of young women than in a refuge for the socially disadvantaged? And what better disguise than to pass as a bountiful patron, picking out young women to act as 'assistants' while they waited for a

184

marriage proposal? She resolved to weigh her words as if they were guineas and to ensure she was never again alone with Lady Arbuthnot.

There was a black-painted door at the end of the corridor and she pushed it, until it gave onto a huge dark space.

"Be careful," she said to Lady A. "This must be the exhibition hall—as I recall, it's very large and there is a raked viewing platform so that people at the rear can see over the heads of those in front. There is probably broken glass too, from the tank."

Lady A made a sound: it could have been assent but Heidi was forced to admit it could equally have been a snort of derision. She let the beam dance across the floor picking out a skim of water, a dropped glove, and the jagged edges of the glass tank. It was difficult to move forward and leave the relative security of the corridor and step into the stygian space of the hall. The only thing that made her do it was the sense that Lady A was waiting impatiently behind her.

Heidi's feet splashed through puddles as she moved out into the emptiness. She led the way into the vast space, hearing her footsteps echo on the stone floor, her skirt's every movement amplified by the empty room until the shirring sound of petticoats was like the nibbling of thousands of tiny insects. Then she kicked something that rattled across the floor, a small clattering something. She bent, chasing it down with the torchlight, and caught a glimpse that wasn't water. Let it be an earring or a brooch she thought. Let it be gold or emeralds and let me get to it and slide it into my reticule before Lady A sees it.

She walked forward, playing the beam of light away from the small shining object and the older woman unconsciously followed the path of the light, moving parallel to Heidi rather than behind her. It was the work of a moment to stoop and grab the item, but once it was in her hand, her fingers found it impossible to identify. She ran her thumb over its surfaces, smooth and cold, yet flexible, like jointed glass, about half as long as her little finger and the same width around. Heidi was nonplussed, turning the finger over and over in her hand.

"It's bigger than I'd thought," Lady A's voice startled her and Heidi looked ahead to the shattered case, like a ruined castle in a fairy tale.

185

"Yes," she replied. "The automaton was pacing around inside, totally submerged in the water."

"How extraordinary," Lady A seemed to be looking at Heidi's hand and there was nothing to do but open her fingers and shine the torch on what she'd picked up. It wasn't a diamond earring or emerald brooch—it was a glass artefact, like a bulb, but thicker and smaller and with a tangle of copper and silver wires inside which looked very much like entrails.

"What on earth is it?" Lady A poked at the object with her fan.

"I don't know. It's a device of some kind, but I can't tell its purpose."

"Devices usually have a handle or switch," declared Lady A. "My grandson has a clockwork monkey with a key, and the torch, as you know, has a switch."

"It's difficult to examine something so small by torchlight," Heidi snapped, but she handed the torch back to its owner and began to turn the object from side to side in the brilliant light Lady A shone into her palm.

"It looks like a prawn," Lady A said.

Heidi frowned.

Lady A went back to her educational voice, "Prawns are not pink when they are alive, you know. You've probably never seen a live one, but they are transparent in their natural habitat."

"Thanks for the lecture," Heidi muttered. Lady A was right though—the glass miniature did resemble a prawn, right down to the bulbous eyes and segmented tail, and as her busy fingers turned it over, she realised the thing was very much like . . . "It's one of the deep sea creatures from the tank!" She grabbed the torch and held the glass object upright in its light, bobbing it along as though it were swimming.

"Don't be ludicrous, child."

"It is!" Heidi insisted. "And if I can just . . . " But no matter how she twisted and shook the glass device it would not light up.

Lady A sniffed and took the torch back, scanning the floor. They found another glass crustacean and the crushed fragments and tangled innards of a third, scattered among the shards of glass from the tank.

"That was my third observation," Heidi said. "The automaton kept telling us that the pressure of water in the depths of the ocean was so great

186

that animals raised to the surface would explode."

"Fish," interjected Lady A. "Not animals, my dear."

Heidi ignored her. "But when the automaton broke the tank, the water didn't burst out, it was just as if somebody had tipped over a hip bath. Surely there was something wrong with what he said, or with the tank?"

"And . . . ?" Lady A seemed to have lost interest. She began to pick her way back to the entrance. Heidi tucked the device into her reticule and followed. She would come back on her own and investigate further.

"Well, I can't imagine we have gained anything by this visit." Lady A said, when they were back in the alley.

"I agree." Heidi wanted to get back to the SSYL and complete the tasks set for every young woman who lodged there.

"Although we have discovered that there are more mysteries than we originally thought." Lady A continued. "First, why was the dead woman in the tank, second, why did the automaton panic and third, those little things." She pointed to Heidi's reticule. "And finally, of course, the mystery of why the pressure of water in the tank was so low, after the machine made such a point of telling you all that it would compress a normal fish until it died?"

Heidi blinked. The old woman had taken the point after all.

"And one more," Lady A began to walk back down the alley. "Why didn't that place smell worse?"

"I beg your pardon?"

"Think of a fishmongers, Heidi. They smell awful at the best of times. Yet we have here a huge quantity of salt water filed with various examples of marine life, all spilled on the floor and left for days and yet it only smells damp, not briny or fishy."

"Somebody's been in to clear up?" Heidi suggested. "They removed all the fish . . . " she slowed. Lady A was right: the piscatorial life she'd seen in the tank had been, for the most part, minute. Nobody could have found every prawn, jellyfish and other tiny creature, and those that had been missed would have developed a stench out of all proportion to their size.

"I'll tell you something else," she continued. "I didn't think of it at the time, but I realise now that it was probably significant. When the automaton got into the tank, it climbed up a ladder and down another that led

187

into a small glass cubicle on the side of the tank. That cubicle had a lid which the machine closed, and then it turned a dial to allow water to enter the space in which it stood.

Lady A snapped her fan again.

"Please don't do that, this is important."

"Do what?"

"Whenever you're bored or impatient you begin to tap your fan. It's most distracting."

"Do I?" The older woman seemed surprised. "Well I'm sorry. Continue."

"It was a dramatic moment, watching the water rise in the cubicle, and the gaslights were lowered slowly as it did, so that by the time the automaton opened the door which gave onto the main tank, things were rather shadowy. But I clearly remember that the water ran into the cubicle like bathwater and surely, if it were of the same intense pressure as the tank—"

"It would have been a jet, like the water cannon they used on those poor Indian protesters who wanted independence," said Lady A. "I was in Delhi and saw the cannonade they used, the crowd was swept away like twigs in a torrent, even the elephants had difficulty keeping their feet. You're right, my dear."

"And so?" Heidi shook her head. "Can we reach any conclusions?"

"I fear not, or not as yet, but our resources are not exhausted. I shall talk to some men of science and see what they make of this conundrum."

Heidi followed her back to the steam carriage and they travelled back in silence. Finally Lady A said, "I shall invite the President of the Royal Society to dine, he will know which scientists are best placed to help us."

Heidi nodded, distracted. Somebody already knew exactly what had been going on at the Vasty Deep and she'd decided to find that person and ask them. Lady A could talk to her eminent friends all she liked, Heidi was convinced the answer lay with the low and silent of society: cleaners and doorkeepers, carriage drivers and maids —all she had to do was find those who'd been employed to care for the exhibition.

◊

The journey to Vasty Deep took four times as long by horse-drawn omnibus. Heidi ignored the front entrance, bowing her head and hunching her shoulders as she scurried to the back of the building, but the entrance she'd used with Lady A was now crudely boarded up. She reached out to check how secure the roughly-nailed wooden slats really were . . .

"Oi!" A high-pitched yell made her jump and she closed her eyes for a moment, dreading what she would see when she turned.

It was as bad as she'd feared. Behind her was a child, half-hidden in a doorway. A nipper, probably between nine and thirteen, and apparently male. She knew that was a deception: nippers could be either sex at will. They were street children, wild and wayward, living in 'warrens' composed only of children and the guards they paid to protect them.

A nipper could cut a throat, or more likely a hamstring, with a razor blade hidden in a bible or a doll, kneel beside the victim and sob like a frightened child while picking the pockets of the rapidly expiring adult. In seconds the nipper would have vanished around a corner or down an alley with its spoils, and if the robbed one survived to try and identify the thief, it was highly likely that the child in question had been dressed in the opposite gender's clothing. All it took was a moment: a dress pulled over britches and a bonnet jammed down on a mop-cut head, or a smock torn off to reveal knickerbockers and a shirt, while collar-length hair was shoved under a boy's cap. Boy became girl, girl-boy. Even in court there was little hope of proving the child had been involved in a crime and if you did, deportation just had them running around Australia like venomous rabbits.

Nippers had no remorse. They possessed a violent loyalty to other members of their warren but no other feelings. They would kill, fight and die with savage ferocity and expose themselves to any danger. And Heidi was alone with one of them.

"I was lookin' for work," she said. "I heard as how a girl died down here and I needs a job."

"Gah!" The child jeered. "Jump in her grave to rob her bones, would ya? She ain't even hardly cold yet."

"I needs a job," Heidi kept her head and voice low, knowing poverty was her only defence. A nipper would cut her up for the price of a pie or a bowl of soup, if it felt like it.

"You don't want her job, you daft mare! She done herself in cos it was so bad." The child moved forward and Heidi saw a pinch-faced boy wearing an outsized velveteen waistcoat, trousers

189

and heavy boots. The boots would hack at the victim's shins until he or she fell over, at which point the wicked blade would be pulled from a waistcoat pocket and drawn across the throat.

"I'm not soft," she whined. "If I don't get work I might as well kill myself an' all."

The nipper sniffed. "Get on with you," he said. "You ain't goin' to get work here, anyway. They've cut and run, them gents what owned it."

Heidi let herself sink to the step. She held her hands over her face but opened her fingers enough to see the nipper, in case it came too close for safety. "What can I do? I needs work." She pretended to sob and shudder. "Where've they gone?"

The nipper shrugged. "Done a flit is all I know. Didn't even pay the last week's wages—there's women round here as'd beat them gents to death as soon as look at them."

"But they'll be startin' up somewhere else, won't they? They're goin' to need workers then . . ."

The nipper tilted his head. "What's it worth?"

She pretended to dig through her bag. "I've got a penny . . . " the child's face didn't change. "A penny farthing then. It's all I've got."

The nipper moved fast, crossing the alley and snatching the money from her fingers before returning to its doorway.;

"Woman called Molly—lives round the corner in the house with the blue door. She worked for 'em as an overseer. She must know somethin'."

Heidi stood and rearranged her shawl, giving the nipper time to disappear, but she could feel his eyes on her as she half-ran round the corner and back into the wider street where there was less risk of attack.

She found the house with the blue door and knocked. Nobody answered. She sat on the greasy step and waited. It grew dark and she began to fear she could see the glowing eyes of a multitude of nippers closing in on her in the encroaching dusk, but her rational self knew it was only rats.

Eventually a shirt-sleeved man strolled up to the door.

"You waitin' for Molly?" he asked as he fitted his key to the grimy lock.

Heidi nodded.

"She'll be another hour. She's been kept late," he said and slammed the door in her face.

It was fully dark when Molly came home and the street, lacking gaslights, had a solid menace to its dark corners. Heidi has spent the last half hour alternately wishing she'd held onto Lady A's torch and remembering that if she had, the nipper would have cut her throat for it as soon as she turned it on.

Molly, with her shawl folded over her head, a jute sack of groceries dangling from one hand and a flattened nose that suggested her husband beat her, did not seem the kind of woman to hand out information. Nor was she. Heidi tried the same approach she'd used with the nipper and got only a sarcastic smile in reply. If she hadn't been blocking the doorway, she doubted Molly would have given her even that much.

She weighed the woman's appearance in her mind: too slovenly to wear a bonnet or carry a shopping bag, but brave or strong enough to be out on the street after dark. The nipper said she'd been an overseer and that meant she'd wielded some power, even if she was powerless against the spousal fist. What made such a woman share information? Not weakness, but strength.

"That woman who died," she said. "I want to know who she was and what happened to her."

Molly leaned against the wall. "Do you? Well, you want a lot. First it's a word with me, then it's a job from me, now it's the ins and outs of somebody else's death. What I want is to know who you are and what you're up to."

Heidi decided she might as well tell everything. Molly would spot any lies and her only chance to win this dour woman over was to offer her back a little of the power she'd lost—the power, at least, to try for revenge on the men who owed her wages.

Molly listened without comment, then sat down on the step beside her.

"I ain't askin' you in," she said. "Because my old man's in there and he's not good company since I lost my job." Her fingers rose and seemed to explore her facial bruising without her knowledge. "The girl what drowned was Florence Altmann. They'd just laid her off as being too slow and she'd got a mum and invalid sister to support, so I s'pose she just couldn't bear going home and telling them she'd lost her job."

191

"What was the job?" Heidi asked.

"You saw the show, didn't you? All those little sea creatures? We made them in a workshop upstairs. Terrible fiddly work, getting all the little bits to fit inside the bodies and Florence just wasn't nimble-fingered enough to please 'em, so they sacked her."

Heidi remembered the little glass object. "They were glass machines?"

"Yeah. Don't ask me why cos I never knew. They didn't pay badly, I'll say that for 'em and I thought I was onto a winner when they put me in charge. I had to test each one lit up properly and then test it again to be sure it was water-tight. About half of them wasn't. It's a difficult job, getting glass to be flexible and waterproof."

Molly sounded proud of her efforts and Heidi saw that the way to reach her was not power, but pride.

"Difficult work," she said.

"I'll tell you how difficult—at first they hired men, thinking they'd master the nano-works best, but men was too clumsy. So then they took on us women, but they never expected us to be much good at it. At the end of the first week I got them to explain it all to me

and then I explained it to the piece-workers and we was off and runnin'. It wasn't so difficult to understand, I don't reckon."

"By why do it in the first place?"

Molly frowned. "That I don't know. It wasn't cheap, I can tell you that. 'Twixt you and me, I sat every week and calculated the wages they paid out against the income from the show and they had to be making a loss, so I was always expecting them to shut the place down, but they never even tried to cut our pay, till they skipped out on us."

"They couldn't shut down," Heidi said. "They had to mount a public exhibition, by law."

"Is that right?" Molly was taken aback. "I never heard that."

Heidi shook her head. "I just don't understand. It was all a big illusion that cost a lot of money and I don't comprehend any of it, but what about Florence? That's what I really want to get to the bottom of."

Molly looked into the distance. "Did you ever know a girl who was doomed?"

Heidi shrugged. "I don't know what you mean."

"Course you do. Not too bright, a little bit clumsy, ugly. Eager to please, but too loud or too quiet all the time, never has a young man, ends up looking after her old mum or her old dad, or her sister's brats . . . "

Heidi nodded. There were such girls in SSYL, destined to be governesses or missionary workers or nurses. They were, in fact, the kind of girls she avoided like a dark alley. A young woman who aimed to succeed could not afford to burden herself with friends who would drag her down—not in Victoria's bustling England where you were judged on how well you were managing your social climb.

"That was Flo," Molly said, tucking her shawl into her armpits and standing. "And that's all I can tell you."

Heidi stood too. "I'll find out," she said. "And I'll come and tell you."

Molly shrugged. "Don't matter to me. Tell me where there's a job for me and I'll thank you, but that's all I'm interested in." She pulled a key from her apron and entered the house, closing the door decisively in Heidi's face.

Heidi checked her reticule again. The money in it was all she had for the rest of the week, but she couldn't bear to take the omnibus and wonder if she was being followed by the feral-eyed nipper and his gang, waiting for the moment to kneecap her. Instead she used every ha'penny to hire a hansom carriage and made sure it stopped in the glare of the gaslight outside SSYL. They would not come after her once they knew she was on the brink of poverty. She'd reached a dead end in her search, but she could at least ensure it became an end, without the dead part.

◊

The next morning, Lady A's carriage was there again, and the chauffer once more called Heidi out of the group.

"I have drawn a blank," said Lady A. "The President was woefully ignorant of young men working in the areas of marine and micro-technology. I told him so. He said he couldn't see the relevance and I told him that as he was supposedly a scientist I found that at least as worrying as his inability to describe what the scientists in his Society were doing." Her eyes lowered to Heidi, standing beside the carriage. "I have a feeling he was deliberately denying knowledge."

Heidi fought the impulse to curtsey. "I too have drawn a blank. I discovered that the dead woman, Florence Altmann, was working as an artificer of the small glass creatures we found, and that she probably drowned herself after losing her job for slowness, but the men who ran the workshop in which she worked and the Vasty Deep itself, appear to have decamped into the night."

Lady A blinked. "You've been remarkably busy. I had no idea you were striking out on your own."

Heidi realised her fee could be at stake. "I knew the woman who ran the workshop would lie if confronted with authority. She would only talk to somebody she believed was desperate for work and willing to connive at illegality —if she'd met you, she'd have clammed up. I was going to telegraph you this morning with the news."

The old woman looked at her for far too long for comfort. "Come along then," she said eventually. "We can meet in the middle. A few steps down the ladder from the President of the Royal Society and a few steps up from the woman you met."

Heidi tightened her bonnet and swung up into the carriage, disdaining the chauffer's proffered hand. "What do you mean?"

Lady A grinned like a skull. "The SSYMP has a young man called Wellyers. Until a few days ago he was employed as the manager of *The* *Wonders of the Vasty Deep*, now he is seeking a bursary from SSYMP to travel to Canada to set up a loggery. He sounds like a young man in a hurry, don't you think?"

Heidi nodded.

"So we are going, as representatives of a charitable committee that supports young men of promise, to see if we would like to fund his prospective career. Doubtless we will want to know a little about his past employment."

Heidi nodded again, not entirely sure what a loggery was, but certain that Lady A would cope magnificently and that she would only need to look demure and listen.

Frederick Wellyers had a small blond moustache and was a bit of a dandy. Heidi could feel her heart softening inside her ribs as she gazed at him, and his eyes strayed occasionally, but meaningfully from Lady A to interrogate Heidi's gaze and suggest romance. She wasn't sure how he was doing this, but she knew he was, and knew she was responding. Lady A knew it too, and became drier and more acerbic each time it happened.

"The gentlemen doubtless had their reasons," Freddy Wellyers said. "But they left me up the creek without a paddle. Without even, one could say, a canoe!" He smiled at his own witticism and Heidi smiled in sympathy. "Not a word of warning, no salary for my final month, nothing. A chap has to move fast to secure a new position, you know. The Giles Parham Association for the Promotion of Civilizing Remote Places have offered me a place in Canada, but no fare."

"Yeeeess." Lady A did a fair impression of an adder hissing a warning. "So you were a manager of an entertainment? Nothing there seems to particularly fit you for the arduous work of running a logging concession."

Freddy smoothed his moustache. "I'm tougher than I look," he said, and Heidi remember saying almost the same thing to the nipper. "The entertainment was not frivolous, it was a display of marine life, intended to show the populace the value of our great marine explorations. So I am equipped to understand the beauties and power of nature, to manage a small team, to exploit the world's resources to the benefit of Empire . . . " he ran out of steam and blinked rapidly. "And I like trees," he finished, somewhat uncertainly."

"This display . . . you say the gentlemen who ran it just disappeared? That doesn't seem likely, or gentlemanly."

Freddy blinked again. "Lord Roleson had to go home as his father has gout, Sir Archimedes Boult was urgently needed in Antigua by another one of his enterprises, His Excellency Sir Roger Vyers was recalled by his regiment and the Honourable Julian Smythe developed a religious conviction and has gone to be confirmed as a Catholic."

Lady A smiled at him, and disconcerted him further. He checked his moustache had not run away, which he seemed quite likely to want to do himself, and shivered slightly. Heidi felt herself shiver too. Poor Freddy, he seemed to be everybody's victim.

"So you were left holding the baby." Lady A's words seemed to shock Freddy, whose mouth opened and closed without speech. "Metaphorically speaking, I mean."

He smiled and nodded. "Yes . . . well, there you are, gentlemen have many demands on their time and talents, and nobody can say why such things happen. So, will your estimable society fund my passage?"

Lady A leaned forward, imposed her skull-like smile between Freddy and Heidi and shook her head. "Oh no, Mr Wellyers. Because if we funded your passage, we would also be funding the continuation of your lies and that would not be in the public interest."

"Lies?" Freddy's voice faltered.

"Let me see . . . the exhibition was a fraud, the workshop above it has not been mentioned, the gentlemen must have taken you into their confidence enough for you to know that what they were doing was venal and wrong, and a young woman drowned herself in the Vasty Deep's tank . . . "

The silence was appalling. Heidi felt her fingers clenching into her fists. Poor Freddy, didn't Lady A understand what it was like to be at the mercy of the world's rich? No, of course she didn't.

Then Lady A spoke again. "And that's without mentioning your own misdoings—there are three orders for maintenance and care out in your name, Mr Wellyers: Frederick Greene, aged twenty-two months, Alice Rotherhide, aged ten months and Alfred Coutstable, aged nine months. You must have been a busy young man to father both Alice and Alfred so close together—did their mothers live in adjoining streets? And

have you considered making an honest woman of any of them?"

Heidi looked down. Her nails had made eight bloody crescents in her palms. That was going to hurt when she had to turn the mangle on laundry duty the next day, and it served her right. She'd nearly fallen into her mother's error, just because a man was as handsome as Narcissus. She lifted her chin and banished her soft heart back to its bony cage. "Molly tells me that you turned Florence Altmann off for being slow at her work. You caused her suicide, in other words—I'm not sure that fits you for any kind of work, Mr Wellyers, and I think we may feel it necessary to ensure every employment agency in England knows it."

Freddy shivered again, but this time Heidi saw it as the weakness it was. He was hollow and rang like a bell to whatever words he'd last heard. Now he fell over himself to tell the truth. "I can only tell you what they told me, which is that some failure in transportation caused them to have to rig the show. They said the real creatures would turn up one day, when the vessel carrying them had been repaired. It wasn't a fraud so much as a . . . delaying tactic."

196

Heidi decided it was time to speak. "You are clearly not the most astute of managers. Somebody else must have been the motive force in the day to day operations. Who was it?"

Freddy blinked at her and then nodded furiously. "You're right, it wasn't me at all. It was the automaton. It was in charge of everything really."

Lady A directed her chauffer to take them to the nearest telegraph office and they travelled in silence. Heidi had been shocked by her gullibility in relation to Freddy and Lady A seemed equally disturbed by the list of names that Freddy had revealed as being part of the Vasty Deep conspiracy.

At the office she ordered a priority cable to be sent to the automata registry and waited impatiently for the reply, fan tapping. Heidi remembered that she had information of her own. "Flo Altmann was supporting a mother and invalid sister. Should you feel you could do anything to help them, I suspect they will be in Whitechapel poorhouse."

Lady A frowned. "Well, I suppose one can organise a small pension. It would be better to reform the poorhouses altogether—they are vile places, but that's a huge task."

Heidi shivered. The poorhouse was her biggest fear.

The pneumatic chute delivered a capsule and the clerk opened it and handed the paper inside to Lady A. It was the address at which the automata was now employed. A slaughterhouse in Lime Street. Lady A offered to take Heidi back to SSYL and for a second she hesitated, knowing that the shambles would be a place of blood and death that would shock even a hardened working woman, but if Lady A could face it, so could she. Anyway, she needed to earn that fee.

It was worse than she had feared. From the other end of the street the bellowing of cows could be heard, over which the shrill whinnies of horses being slaughtered rang like broken trumpets. The carriage stopped outside the heavy wooden gates and for the first time, Lady A appeared unable to cope and sat back in her seat, fanning herself. "I'm a vegetarian," she said. "Mr George Bernard Shaw convinced me that eating meat was an indecency several years ago."

Heidi didn't mention that the horses were going to be rendered, not consumed, instead she picked up the speaking tube and asked the chauffer to take them back to the far end of the street and then to walk down and tell the slaughterhouse foreman that Lady Arbuthnot needed to examine the automaton's work record. "Allow them to believe she's from the register, without actually saying so," Heidi instructed him. The man nodded.

When the automaton appeared outside the carriage, it was splashed from foot to waist with blood. It was, as Heidi remembered, one of the smooth-faced versions, with chiselled lips and a small straight nose, but lacking the bronzed hair and beard that the latest automata sported. In its hand it held the brass tube that contained the punched metal record of its employment.

Lady A looked on it with as much distaste as Heidi but took the tube and emptied it into her lap, shaking out the steel wafers and shuffling them as if she could actually read their cryptograms. "You were at the Vasty Deep," she said.

The automaton couldn't blink, but the immobility of its face somehow conveyed panic. It looked at her, then at Heidi and failed to speak.

"Speak when you are addressed," Lady A was getting into her stride. "What were your duties there?"

The machine waved its hand elegantly, but didn't look away from Heidi. "As you can see on my wafer."

Lady A was not fazed by this. "Ah, but it seems that you were regularly exceeding your listed duties. Do you deny it?"

The automaton drooped. "I cannot deny it. The young lady saw me. I opened the exhibit without permission. I exceeded my duties."

"That is an infraction that could result in disassembly," Lady A said. The automaton drooped further, until it looked already broken.

"But it is possible you can be given some leniency, if you can help us with another matter."

The machine turned its head impossibly over its shoulder to stare at the slaughterhouse. "It might be better to return to my component parts."

"Your choice entirely," Lady A countered.

Eventually the automaton straightened. "I shall help in whatever way I can. And hope for some em

ployment better than this . . . " its hand waved towards the shambles.

"I shall promise nothing," Lady A said. "But cooperation will be taken into account."

It nodded. "Then you will wish to know two things: the first is that the gentlemen that bid successfully to become the Marine Exploration Consortium have been selling shares and debentures in their marine prospecting to the total sum of . . . " it froze momentarily while it calculated, a fricative rasp coming from its cogs and fluid connectors, " . . . seven million pounds sterling."

Heidi gasped. "How much?"

The automaton looked at her. "Enough to buy the Isle of Man."

Lady A seemed to be struggling to find words. "What is the other thing?"

"The other thing is that the ship that is supposed to be exploring the deep oceans doesn't exist."

Lady A's fan fell out of the carriage window. The automaton stooped and picked it up but Lady A waved the mud-spattered accessory away. "Doesn't exist?"

The machine shook its head. "I asked about insurance for the vessel. It was my responsibility to tally the income and outgoings, and there appeared to be no insurance premium on the ship's voyages. The consortium told me it was something they were paying privately, but when I checked with Lloyd's Register, the ship did not exist."

"And you did nothing?" Lady A thundered.

"I did not want to be disassembled."

Heidi nodded. She knew the risks of honesty—for once she was on an automaton's side.

◊

Lady A dropped her back at SYLL. The next afternoon the chauffer turned up and handed Heidi a beautifully embossed envelope with a large green wax seal on which was imprinted the Arbuthnot crest. Heidi resisted the temptation to bob her knee like a housemaid and waited until she got to her room to open it. There was a banker's draft for ten guineas inside.

She knew what that meant. Lady A had been willing to snoop and pry when it was a matter of bullying machines or weak young men, or browbeating a scientist known to be terrified of society dowagers, but when it came to confronting leaders of society, even if they had defrauded the public of seven million pounds of failed hopes and lost investments, the old lady was withdrawing from the fight. She'd been paid off.

199

Heidi took her draft and cashed it. She bought a merino shawl and twelve yards of top quality wool cloth in shades of blue and grey and a good strong travelling case. She caught an omnibus down to the stop nearest Vasty Deep and banged on Molly's door.

"Here," Heidi said, when the other woman appeared. "A guinea. For helping me."

Molly nodded. "You got what you wanted then?"

Heidi shook her head. "No, but I got something, which is more than poor Flo did."

Molly nodded again. "Take care of yourself, girl."

"I am," Heidi lifted her chin. "Don't you worry, I am."

Back at SYLL she put her fabrics in the case along with her few other possessions, wrapped the shawl around her shoulders, and ordered a steam taxi to taker her to SSYMP. On the way she stopped at her bank and drew out her pathetic life savings.

"Mr Wellyers," she demanded of the SSYMP doorman. "Please send him down immediately."

Freddy soon appeared, smoothing his hair and tugging down his cuffs. Heidi remembered how Lady A had done it, and leaned on the taxi window, snapping her fan. "My Wellyers," she said. "You're a sad excuse for a gentleman."

Freddy nodded.

"An innocent woman would be mad to throw her lot in with you."

He nodded again.

"But I'm not an innocent, and I'm not throwing my lot. I'm offering you a chance. But you'll have to meet my conditions now, and every day, for the rest of your life."

He gazed at her for a long time, before asking, "What conditions?"

"First, you'll marry me. Second, I'll cover our fare to Canada, and you'll make a signed testament that in consideration of my investment, all future incoming finance is to be transferred immediately and without prejudice to me, while all debts incurred by you remain your sole and single responsibility."

She watched his thoughts move across his face. It was the opposite of the Vasty Deep, she thought. There, the darkness had been illuminated by tiny shards of beauty, here was beauty darkened by spatters of fear, cunning and weakness. But one thing was the same in both cases. Deception. She had to break through his charm if they were to have any chance at all.

She leaned forward. "Freddy, I don't love you, and you don't love me. But we've got a chance to get out of here and perhaps make a go of things. I promise you I'll be a good wife as long as you don't father any more bastards, but if you do, I'll poison you. With your manners and my wits, well . . . perhaps one day we could buy the Isle of Man."

He leaned into the carriage. "I don't know your name, even."

She heard the warmth in his tone and knew he was going to take the gamble. Better a weak husband than none at all, and better a charming man in Canada, away from temptation than a dolt in London, immune to it. She could make something of Freddy, she was sure of it.

"Heidi Naismith, soon to be Wellyers," she replied. "Come on, there's a steamer sailing to Quebec in three days and we should be married and on it. We'll send the taxi back for your traps, let's go and find a minister who'll marry us in a hurry."

He opened the taxi door and saw her travelling case. "You were mightily confident of my response," he said.

Heidi shook her head. "I was going anyway, with you or without."

As the taxi pulled away she turned to look out over the Thames, wondering if Lady A was somewhere out there, pretending to be a detective again. Good luck to the old duck, but Heidi wasn't going to fall for that altruistic rubbish. London ate people alive, and the only way to stop it was to bite first. She opened her mouth carnivorously wide and snapped a chunk out of the twilight sky. Freddy stared at her. "Don't worry," she said. "I'm just saying goodbye to the old city."

THE END

CANCER

FRED VENTURINI

D o not be a voyeur if you are not a Cancer; you have no business with Cancer's private matters today. If you are a Cancer, you have below average height, with an athletic body and short legs. The build should allow for a strong, confident person, but you are not. Despite your brown hair, well-defined face, tan complexion, prominent forehead, and full mouth with full lips, you cannot contain the gloom inside you. That gloom, much like your love, is held like water in your hands leaking from the seams of your flesh you can't close tight enough because they are you.

Your ex-wife is not in intensive care anymore, but she remains in the coma, and her eyes open once in a while and she tries to talk, but the brain damage is too severe. She will never speak again. The loving, emotional, loyal, generous, wise, romantic, warm, sympathetic side of you hates to see her in such a state. Being divorced, you can't make any final decisions for her.

Teri senses that warmth inside of you. She doesn't mind when you introduce her as your girlfriend because of that warmth, yet senses you are changeable, moody, devious, clinging, indecisive, and insecure.

Tell her you surf "committed-only" dating sites and kept your old wedding band for these encounters. Throw that noble brick through her window and watch the blood soak into rough stone. Tell her that the night she surprised you with take-out from China Pearl, the night she made love to you for the third time in the history of your relationship, you had screwed a fifty-four year old married woman named Nancy in the back of her Inifiniti SUV earlier in the day. Even you could smell Nancy all over you, her lingering breath on your lips, her perfume on your skin. You ate the Chinese and watched a movie and kissed Teri goodbye. You even said you had missed her all day. She left without looking back at you, and it was then you feared it wouldn't last.

But you don't read this to know what has already happened. You want to know the future. You want vague, fortune-cookie lines that can be molded into life preservers of love, happiness, and luck, but you must not be enabled by the vague optimism that betrays the true, scientific nature of astrology.

Teri will not return your calls. You will never see her again. It is your fault.

The inevitable weaknesses of Cancer are glossy beads, easily seen, that never drip away.

Tonight: Do not use rope. Put towels around the crevices of your garage where air can escape. You're nodding now, and crying, and will try to leave a note but Teri won't read it; she is a Virgo and will not shed one tear.

THE END

POLLUTO.

The Guilty Parties
or
Contributor Bios

Forrest Aguirre's fiction has appeared in a variety of venues, including, most recently *Asimov's* and *Farrago's Wainscot* and is forthcoming in *Clockwork Phoenix, Hatter Bones,* and *Avant-garde for the New Millenium.* He won the World Fantasy Award for editing the *Leviathan 3* anthology with Jeff VanderMeer.

Kelly Barnhill is a teacher, writer and mama, living in the frozen heart of North America. Her previous work has appeared in *Postscripts, Weird Tales, Underground Voices* and in Ann and Jeff Vandermeer's new anthology, *Fast Ships Black Sails.* Additionally, her first novel, a YA fantasy called *The Boy Without a Face,* is due to be released by Little Brown in the spring of 2010.

Philippa Bower won the fourth Linghams Short Story Competition in 2006 and lives in East Preston, UK. Demons live in her attic and trolls live on toadstools in her basement. Occasionally the two forces battle for control of the kitchen, but Philippa manages to weigh in with her rolling pin and restore equilibrium. This way she never does any chores herself.

Kristina Marie Darling is the author of several small press collections of poetry and nonfiction, including *Fevers and Clocks* (March Street Press, 2006), *The Traffic in Women* (Dancing Girl Press, 2006), *Night Music* (BlazeVox Books, 2008), and, most recently, *Strange Gospels* (Maverick Duck Press, 2009).

Mark Howard Jones lives in Cardiff and has had dozens of stories published here, there and somewhere. His novella *The Garden of Doubt on the Island of Shadows* is now available from Manchester's ISMS Press.

Ren Holton is the alter ego of another, nicer, writer. Ren is the person people never invite to parties, but always speak to when they want a dubious favour. Despite this, Ren manages an almost autonomous existence and can be found within, but separate to, reality. Recent Ren Holton works have been published in *SciFantastic, Deathgrip: Exit Laughing, Shadow Plays* and at *The Late Late Show*, and are forthcoming in *North of Infinity* and *Strange Pleasures #6.*

Deb Hoag is the author of *Crashin' the Real* and has become something of a mascot at *Polluto.* Her second novel is the tale of what happens to Dracula when he visits Freud, and is due out next year from Dog Horn Publishing.

POLLUTO.

Rhys Hughes is a sordid genius. Or a word-playing savant. Or a strange little Welsh man who makes penises out of wine gums on beaches. His next collection, *Mister Gum*, is due out from some insane publisher willing to touch it. Erm, that is, us!

Kurt Kirchmeier is from Canada. He has a very strange name. Currently his identity has been stolen by a super-evolutionary chick from Alpha Centauri. Maybe one day he'll get it back.

Miles Klee lives and works in Hell's Kitchen, New York City, but grew up in the utter weirdness of New Jersey. He studied creative writing intensively under acclaimed authors Jim Shepard and Andrea Barrett. His fiction has been featured in *McSweeney's Internet Tendency* and *Yankee Pot Roast* and will appear in an upcoming issue of *Birkensnake*.

Mr Kuch's creative writing credits include *Commonweal, North American Review, Slow Trains, Slant, Thema, Timber Creek Review*, and other periodicals. He participated in a Mid-American Review Summer Fiction Workshop, and has taken several courses at the Writers Center, Bethesda, Maryland. As a computer systems consultant, he has travelled five continents and 35 countries. He lives in Falls Church, Virginia, with his wife and three cats.

Robert Lamb has been a very bad boy. Please excuse him.

Dave Migman scares us. A lot. His first novel, *The Wolf Stepped Out*, is perhaps due out for Halloween, but we're too terrified to read it.

William Peacock is the author of poetry and stories that have appeared or are forthcoming in *Bat City Review, ESC! Magazine, Diet Soap, Swill*, and elsewhere. As far as ultraviolence and alternate histories go, this bad boy has experienced it all. Indeed, he busted out of Jack Yeovil's Dark Future/ *Demon Download* books some years ago. We're still trying to cram him back in, along with those members of the Diogenes Club to have escaped that same author's *Anno Dracula* books. See why you shouldn't complain about our late response times?

Jon Peck makes his home in the various coffeeshops of the Pacific Northwest, listening in on others' conversations. Read his musings at JonPeck.com and add to (or steal from) his speculative fiction idea-repository at TakeOneDaily.com.

POLLUTO.

Tomas Sanchez Prunier drinks too much moloko. Twisted bastard.

Steve Redwood is a satirist extraordinaire who buggered off Spain for his better health (and our own). Check out his collection *Broken Symmetries*, due out later this year.

J. Michael Shell's fiction has appeared in *Southern Fried Weirdness '07*, *Bound For Evil* (Dead Letter Press), *Subatomic1*, *Space and Time, Tropic: The Sunday Magazine of the Miami Herald*, *Ballista*, *Skive*, *Sounds of the Night*, *Tabard Inn*, *The Benefactor*, and the Not-One-Of-Us Magazine special collection (Going Going) Gone.

Helena Thompson is represented by United Agents. She writes widely and prolifically, including poetry and drama. She uses a stiletto to get what she wants and she peels oranges with it between heists.

Fred Ventorini completed a B.S. in English and Journalism at MacMurray College in 2002, and is currently in the midst of the M.F.A. program at Lindenwood University. His fiction has appeared in *Sinister Tales*, *Truth Magazine*, *Writer's Post Journal*, *Susurrus*, and *Skyline Magazine*.

Deborah Walker lives in London with her two lovely, yet distracting children. She has recently had acceptances from *AlienSkin*, *Atomjack*, *Bards and Sages*, *55 Stitches*, *Arkham Tales*, *Sonar 4*, *Golden Visions*, *Drunk and Lonely Men*, *Absent Willow Review*, and *Poe Little Thing*.

Drew Rhys White is a 2007 graduate of the Clarion Writing Workshop at UC San Diego. This summer, two of his essays appeared in *Geez* magazine's *30 Sermons You'd Never Hear In Church*. His story, "The Accomplished Birder's Guide to Overcoming Rejection," will appear in Jeff VanderMeer's *Last Drink Bird Head* anthology. In October, his play, *Another Night With the Hendricksens*, was featured in the Players Theatre Horror Festival in New York City.

Erik Williams has had short stories published at *Apex Online*, *Dark Recesses Press*, and *GUD*. Not a large list of accomplishments but his wife seems impressed.

Polluto is in no way responsible for its own output and is compiled entirely by loose mental patients. Don't tell Pescadero where we are!

ND - #0492 - 270225 - C0 - 234/156/17 - PB - 9780955063176 - Gloss Lamination